# A NOT SO PURRFECT HEX

## A COTSWOLD CAT FAMILIAR COZY MYSTERY

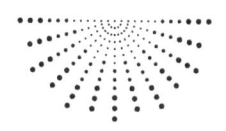

### D. WATTS

Copyright © 2021 by D. Watts

All rights reserved.

No part of this book may be reproduced in any form or by any electronic or mechanical means, including information storage and retrieval systems, without written permission from the author, except for the use of brief quotations in a book review.

Cover Art by Daniela Colleo of StunningBookCovers.com

ABOUT THIS BOOK

**Now, it seems her foes are more fur-midable than ever...**

Felicity Knight always tries to mind her own business, but coming to grips with being a witch makes total neutrality quite the trick...and that's not to mention her untimely penchant for stumbling onto crime scenes.

When Felicity and her father, George, discover the body of a woman (whose local witch tour was followed by true horror), resistance is futile. It's a case that must be cracked.

As if a new murder mystery isn't enough for Felicity and her feline familiar, Atticus, something strange is brewing

ABOUT THIS BOOK

at The River Inn and needs attention. Spirits, however, prove stubborn, and addressing a haunting is daunting.

Meanwhile, the fae are closing in, and danger lurks at every turn, but what could be Felicity's connection to the Fae Queen, Cordelia? Then, there's Mason Reed, a handsome, wholly *charming* wizard. If Felicity stands to trust again, this man may light the way.

Ready for another *tail* of intrigue, and sorcery? It's time to be enchanted!

**A Not So Purrfect Hex** is the third installment of D. Watts' Cotswold Cat Familiar Cozy Mystery Series.

## CHAPTER ONE

"Oh, excuse me," I said, smiling at the older woman, who I'd accidentally bumped into. I held the two glasses I was holding away from her as I looked over her clothes. "I'm so sorry, I didn't splash anything on you, did I?"

The woman smiled kindly, her grey eyes twinkling at me. She looked to be in her seventies, but her face was smooth and practically line free. Her silver hair was swept up in a chignon, which drew attention to the gorgeous, diamond stud earrings she was wearing. A fleeting thought passed over me that I hoped I would look as elegant when I grew older.

"No, I'm quite alright my love, but thanks for asking." She turned her head to where my friends, Darcey, Emma and Mia were sitting at the table. I'm not sure they realised the attention they were drawing to themselves. Each one had a different look but were all aesthetically blessed. Mia's long brown hair was tied up in a high ponytail, with a smattering of light make-up which made her look even younger than her twenty-eight years. Emma had changed the ends of her white, blonde hair - last time I saw her she had them tinted purple but now they were a neon pink which suited her bohemian style. Today she was wearing a flowing black dress, with her signature chunky boots - this particular pair were a patent pink. And lastly, there was Darcey. She had on a pair of knee-high white boots, and a tweed black and white mini dress. Darcey always looked healthy with her lovely olive complexion that set off her black wavy hair, which she wore loosely over her shoulders. She looked like she had walked off an advert for Chanel. And like me, they were also witches.

"You girls look like you're having a good catch up. Go on back to them, I'm fine." She winked at me and I smiled warmly back at her.

"Thanks." I walked back to my table and threw one more glance at her over my shoulder. She had her back to me as she leaned forward to place her order with Nick, the owner of the Mystical Moon pub that we were in. I liked the red blazer she was wearing; it was nice to see some bright colour on this miserable January afternoon.

"Here, you go. One lemonade and orange juice." I pushed it towards Mia. Both Darcey and Emma were indulging in a glass of white wine, but Mia and I opted for a soft drink. Especially as I was on a quick lunch break and had to return to my shop, *All That Glitters.*

"Thanks." Mia took the glass and took a deep swig. I did the same with mine as I settled into my seat.

"Thanks for coming over here to meet me." I smiled at my friends. I had met them on New Year's Eve, three weeks ago, and we'd stayed in contact since then. Emma had set up a group on WhatsApp for the three of us, so there was daily correspondence. Even though I lived here in the village of Agnes, while they currently resided in Oxford which was half an hour away, it felt like I'd known them forever.

"It's no problem, we wanted to see you." Darcey replied. She tossed her hair over her shoulder. "Plus, as you know, we were in Lawnes anyway."

Emma pulled a face and took a sip of her wine.

"I take it you've had no luck then with the house hunt?"

Emma shook her head. "Unfortunately, not.

Mia looked over at Emma and Darcey, with a sudden smile on her face. "Shall we tell her our news?

"Tell me what?" I asked.

"Well, we're thinking about pooling our money

together and buying our own place. After all, not many landlords are happy to take on three cats as well."

I nodded. Pets and landlords weren't always the best combination. "That'd be fantastic if you guys can pool your resources together."

Mia was an accountant and Emma, a graphic designer. Darcey worked as a store manager in a high-end fashion boutique in Oxford. So, between the three of them, I was sure they'd be able to buy something nice. "So, are you thinking about buying in Lawnes, or would you settle in Oxford?" I grinned. "Please say, Lawnes?"

"We're thinking, Lawnes," Emma smiled. "We quite like it, there are some nicer areas and we'd be right next door to you here, in Agnes. I mean, as much as we'd like to buy in this village, the prices are a little out of our reach." She smirked at Mia. "Plus, lover boy, James, will be even closer by."

A deep blush spread across Mia's face.

I elbowed her. "Have you agreed to forgive him yet?"

James was a werewolf shifter who lived in Lawnes. Unfortunately, he cheated on Mia a month ago with a succubus named, Nicky. Mia was heartbroken but James swore blind that Nicky had somehow tricked him. After the New Year's Eve party, we all attended, James had been in touch with Mia daily, begging for her forgiveness. She told us that she realised she missed him just as much but was also happy to make him sweat for a little longer before she'd relent.

"I'm almost there," she replied. "After the latest delivery of roses, I think it may be time to put him out of his misery."

"Or not?" Emma replied. "Our house has never smelt so good with all the flowers she's received."

"True," Mia replied. "I'm going to miss the every-other day delivery."

Darcey looked at her watch. "Oh gosh, is that the time? Ugh, I promised my Mum I'd stop in to see her this afternoon. She's visiting." She rolled her eyes.

Darcey had an interesting relationship with her parents. They'd long split up but were some somehow still the best of friends with each other.

"She's back from Lisbon?" I took another sip of my drink.

"Yup. Apparently for a few days. Staying at dad's and then flying back next week sometime. But she's got some samples for me. That's the best part about the visit." She grinned and took a swig of her wine.

Darcey's mum, Angelina, was a highly successful fashion buyer for a large department store in London. It was easy to see where Darcey inherited her great fashion sense. She told me time and time again that Angelina had offered to get her a job in London, but Darcey was adamant that she wanted to make it on her own.

"Sounds exciting. Do you need to leave now?" I also looked at my watch. I had about half hour before I was due back. My neck started to itch, and I rubbed the spot over the bandage I still had to wear.

"Not just yet," Darcey replied. She motioned with her chin, at my neck. "Still healing alright?"

"Yep, just at that horribly itchy stage." I tugged at my bandage. "Ugh, I can't wait to get this off tomorrow."

"Are you sure you're not a hybrid now?" Mia whispered, feigning mock-horror.

"You mean a half-vamp?" I whispered back. "No, rest assured." A shiver ran up my spine as I replayed that night a few weeks ago, when Raphael bit me. "Mason got all the poison out."

I averted my eyes to my glass. The thought of Mason sent a thrill through me, but I hurriedly pushed the thought away. Two reasons. For one, I was terrible with relationships as they always ended badly. Take Benedict for instance. Case in point. Although to be fair, he had used glamour and a potion on me, but still. Secondly, while Mason was very, very easy on the eye, and had a great personality to match, I'd made a promise to myself to be on my own for the time being. Well, I had Atticus, my familiar, so technically I wasn't completely single.

Also, there was the giant fact that Darcey had a major crush on him.

Mia nudged me. "We think he likes you. A lot."

I snapped my eyes up and looked at Darcey. She winked at me. "He's all yours. I can see that he's completely into you." She drained her wine. "I'm fine, honestly. Besides, I've got my eye on someone else."

I groaned and lowered my head into my hands. "I'm not looking for a relationship. We're just friends."

"Try telling him that," Emma smirked.

"I have," I protested. "Anyway, can we change the subject, please?" I felt heat spread across my face. My friends looked at each other and grinned.

Emma cleared her throat. "Okay, onto official business." She glanced around and lowered her voice. "Lara has given us the go-ahead to try and banish the spirit at The River Inn."

Shortly after New Year, Lara Motley, the current joint head of the Magic Council, and I had encountered a particularly malevolent spirit which had attached itself to The River Inn B&B. I hadn't come across a spectre before, but according to Lara, this one was rather powerful and hostile. She had tried to banish it herself but hadn't realised how strong it was - especially since it had managed to evade her spell and toss her out the window.

I bobbed my head. "Okay, good. I know she was

worried about putting one of us in danger but seems like you convinced her to let you try."

Mia leaned forward. "Absolutely. We were thinking to combine our magic together. Are you in?"

"Most definitely. When?"

"Two days?" Emma suggested. "We need to gather some bits together first." She opened her purse and passed me a piece of paper. Across it was scrawled a spell along with a list of magical items.

"Do you have all this stuff?" I asked, scanning the list once again.

"No, we still need this and this." She pointed to a couple of items on the list.

"Let me get them. I'll pop into *Free Spirits* later. I'm sure Lara will have all this in the back."

"Sounds good." Emma replied. We finished up our drinks and finalised the plan.

CHAPTER TWO

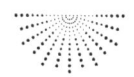

After we left The Mystical Moon, I headed back down the side lane and entered the main village square. From here, I turned right and walked the few yards to my crystal jewellery shop, *All That Glitters.* After I had been bitten by Raphael, the horrid vampire, I had to heal for a week, during which time I had to close my shop. The only thing I could be grateful for was that it was just after Christmas and the shops were quieter in general. Now that we were gearing up to Valentine's day in a couple of weeks' time, I was expecting to get busier with customers wanting gifts for their loved ones.

I entered my shop, flipped the sign around and peeled off my coat.

"Atticus, are you here?" I called for him up the stairs,

which was at the back of my shop. "I'm back." I hung my coat up on the peg and smoothed out my hair.

"Ah, you're back at last. I'm famished."

I glanced up to see my familiar looking down the stairs at me.

"It's barely two o'clock. I thought you had all that leftover chicken for breakfast?"

"Note the semantics of your words, my dear. Emphasis on the word, *breakfast*. My stomach tells me it's past lunchtime now."

I sighed heavily. Sometimes I couldn't win with this cat. I shot a quick glance at the door to check for any incoming customers, but the square was rather quiet. It had rained heavily while I was in the pub, so I presumed most people were indoors somewhere.

I took the stairs two at the time to my flat at the top of the shop and rushed into the small kitchen. I pulled open the fridge.

"What do you fancy? I've got spring tuna from a can. And a little bit leftover of the salmon we had two nights ago."

"Is the tuna human grade?"

I closed the fridge and turned my eyes upwards. "Yes."

"In that case, that should be acceptable."

"Good, because I was hoping to eat the salmon for dinner."

A NOT SO PURRFECT HEX

I pulled open the cupboard and grabbed the tin of tuna. Then I pulled out a plate and spoon and dished it out.

"I've got to get back downstairs. Will there be anything else or do you think you can survive for now?"

Atticus tipped his head up to me. His narrowed eyes and expression implied that he may as well be looking down his nose at me. "Sarcasm is the lowest form of wit." Then he ducked his head and began to eat.

My jaw slackened. Nonetheless I didn't have time for his neurosis, since he very well knew that he was the undefeated King of Sarcasm around here.

A little while later, Luca Rossini, the werewolf shifter from the next town of Lawnes, popped into my shop. Tagging behind him, was James. Luca flashed me a warm grin. Not only was he seeing my friend Lara, but both of them were the current joint heads of The Magic Council in this area.

"Luca. How nice to see you. And you too, James."

Luca made sure to close the shop from the wind and rubbed his hands together. I noted his beard was a little longer than the last time I saw him, but it still suited his face. Plus, being head of a were-shifter crew, I think I'd find it strange to see him clean shaven. His six-foot three frame towered over me. James moved forward pushing his light brown hair out of his eyes. He seemed a little hesitant, possibly because of my friendship with Mia.

"What can I do for you both?"

Luca moved towards my display cabinet. "Hello Felicity. I was hoping I could seek your assistance with a ring for Lara. But you must promise not to tell her."

I nodded, a smile stretching across my face. "Of course. Is it a general gift…or a *special* ring, for a *special* proposal?"

Luca laughed, a deep sound coming from his chest. "It's a special, *special* ring." He winked.

I threw my hand across my mouth, trying to stop my grin from splitting my face. While they hadn't been seeing each other for awfully long, it was obvious just how much they were in love.

"Oh, my stars. Luca, I'm so happy for you!"

He held out his hands to me in mock surrender. "She hasn't said yes, yet."

"I'm sure she will. Do you have anything in mind? What sort of stone you're looking for?"

I was honoured that Luca wanted to buy a piece of jewellery from me. He could have easily gone into Oxford to one of the more traditional jewellery stores.

"Her favourite colour is green. So, perhaps you could help me with some suggestions?"

"Of course. How about I put together some designs for

you this week and you can tell me what you like best, and we go from there?"

He nodded. "Yes, that's what I was hoping for. I'd like something custom made and I think I'll know the one once I see it. Thank you, Felicity."

"My absolute pleasure. How about you, James? Do you need anything?"

He cleared his throat. "I, um, was thinking about getting Mia a necklace for Valentine's Day."

"I'm sure she'd love that."

He looked at Luca who gave him a little nod. "We're still, you know, trying to work things out, but I know she loves that bracelet you made her."

"You mean the silver and rose quartz one?"

"Yeah, that's it. Do you think you could make her a fancy necklace to match?"

I smiled. "Of course, I would be delighted."

He looked to the floor and I genuinely felt sorry for him. He'd made a very stupid mistake, but he was paying a heavy price now. It was clear how much he cared for Mia.

"Thank you," he said, heading for the door.

"My pleasure. Thank you both for stopping in. Luca, I'll be in touch in a few days with some drawings."

"I appreciate it." He gave me a two-finger salute and then they both left the shop.

"What are you doing?" I looked up from my sketchbook to see Atticus stretching out his paws, his mouth open in a huge yawn.

"Oh, hello." I turned back to my book and cocked my head, critically eying the drawings of the few designs I'd sketched for Lara's ring, in between customers. "I'm trying to come up with some unique ideas."

"For Lara's ring?"

I whipped my head to him. "How did you know?"

"I may be snoozing, but my hearing is perfectly fine. I tend to tune you out unless it's something relatively interesting."

"You mustn't tell anyone," I warned him. "Luca wants this to be a surprise."

"I think I've proven you can trust me." Atticus replied haughtily.

I rolled my eyes. "You know what I mean."

He strolled forward and jumped up onto my cabinet, peering at my book.

"Have you thought about the crystal you're going to use?"

I nodded. "Yes, I'm thinking, aventurine."

"Explain."

I placed my pencil down and gave him my full attention. "It's a green crystal, which is what Luca wanted. Aventurine brings good luck and fortune, but also attracts true love and friendships. I think it's the perfect engagement stone. I'll set in in a gold band as it will complement the colour well."

"Actually sounds quite nice."

"I'm glad you approve. I'm still playing around with the style of the band, but I'm really excited to create this." I snapped my book closed and stood up to flick the sign over on my shop. Another day over.

"I'm going to head over to Lara's to pick up a couple of things. Do you want to come?"

"Sure, I could do with a walk."

I quickly did the close down procedure and then grabbed my coat from the peg. It was dark outside but at least it wasn't raining.

As we stepped out into the cool air, it had begun to lightly drizzle. "Come on, let's hurry."

Atticus stepped beside me and we quickly made our way across the square to Lara's shop. She had been out of the country the past week with visiting her suppliers, so it would be good to see her.

Lara hadn't closed the shop yet, so we stepped inside, and I shut the door behind us to keep out the draught. A lovely smell greeted us, akin to roses. I sniffed the air and then noticed she was burning incense sticks by her counter.

"Lara, it's only us." I called out.

She looked up and a large smile spread across her face. "Felicity. How lovely to see you both." She smiled at Atticus. "Come on in. I'm actually supposed to be shut now, but I lost track of the time. Could you turn the sign over, please?"

"Of course." Once I did that, we walked over to her. Limerick, her tawny owl familiar, flew out from the back room and landed softly on Lara's shoulder.

"Hello, Limerick."

"Felicity. Atticus. Tráthnóna maith."

I stared at him blankly.

Lara waved her hand dismissively. "He means *good evening*. He's just showing off by speaking Irish."

Of course. Silly me. Just regular conversation with a talking, Irish owl.

CHAPTER THREE

"So, how are you? I see your wound is almost healed."

I automatically brought my hand up to the side of my neck. "Yes, it is. Bandage is coming off tomorrow. How did you know?"

She merely winked. "I can tell."

I pulled out a stool near her counter and took a seat. Atticus moved away towards the front of the shop. I don't think the incense was going down too well with him.

"I love that smell, what is it?"

She pulled out a packet from behind the counter. "I bought them from Germany. Do you like the scent? I've only just lit them as I didn't want to risk upsetting any customers with allergies, or anything like that."

I nodded, inhaling deeply. "I love it, and I'd buy a pack

in a heartbeat, but…." I glanced over at Atticus. "I don't think Sir would approve."

She chuckled. "Yes, sometimes these things can be too strong. I'm lucky that Limerick puts up with me."

I smiled. Inside I was grinning. If only she knew that Luca was going to propose.

"So, how was Germany?"

"Yes, fine. I need a new shipment of wands, but my supplier was having some trouble with materials. Sometimes it easier to just fly over and figure things out together."

"All sorted now?"

"Oh, yes. How are you getting on with your wand?"

"I love it, thank you. I feel as though it's bonding with me, if that makes sense? It feels a lot more intuitive when I practice with it now."

"That sounds great. All on the right track."

"Well, I won't keep you too long as I'm sure you have plans to get home." I pulled out my phone and opened the picture I'd snapped of Emma's list. "Emma told me earlier that you are happy for us to try and banish the spectre at The River Inn?"

She frowned. "More like she cajoled me. But yes, I relented as long as you're all binding your magic together. I don't want any of you to get hurt."

I pushed the phone towards her. "I understand. Emma

is still missing these items from the spell." I pointed them out to her. One was an oil I hadn't heard of before and the second item were some herbs.

Lara dipped her head. "Yes, I've got these. Let me just grab them from the back." She stood up and Limerick flew off her shoulder to the live branch at the side of the shop. "As you can imagine, some items aren't for public sale in the shop. Give me a couple of minutes."

"Sure, take your time."

Lara disappeared behind her black velvet curtain and I glanced around the shop for a moment and then picked up my phone. I was about to check my Etsy shop, which I now operated on an intermittent basis since I had my shop, when there was a knock on the main door. I glanced up and my breath hitched.

Mason Reed was standing at the door. He raised his hand in a wave.

I got up from my stool and moved to the front door, opening the lock. As soon as I did, Blaze, his golden retriever familiar, bounded towards me, his tail wagging from side to side.

I couldn't help but laugh at his enthusiasm. "Blaze, hello to you too!" I gave a little kiss on his head and then felt Atticus by my ankle, looking up at me. I reached down and petted his head too.

"Atticus." Blaze said in his deep voice, nodding at him.

"Blaze Reed." Atticus replied in a cooler tone.

I caught Mason's eye and smiled. Atticus was a little jealous of the attention I always got from Blaze.

"Hi, Mason," I said.

He pushed his dark blonde hair away from his aqua eyes and adjusted his leather jacket. In his hand, he carried his helmet, which told me he'd ridden his Harley over here.

"Hello, Felicity. I wasn't expecting to see you here, but what a nice surprise."

I moved out of the way and he entered the shop.

"Are you looking for Lara? She's just gone in the back to grab me a couple of items.'

"Yeah, no worries. What are you up to? Plotting something?"

I smiled. "In actual fact, Lara has agreed to let Mia, Emma, Darcey and myself try and banish the spectre at The River Inn.

His smile stilled. "Are you sure that's not too dangerous? I heard about what happened with Lara."

"I know…but we're going to join our magic together. I'm fairly sure that between the four of us, we can do some good magic."

He frowned. "I don't doubt your abilities, but I've heard it's nasty. Do you want some additional help?"

"Not at the minute. But thank you."

I locked eyes with him, trying to read what he was feeling. Mason had taught me to shield my thoughts - and I'm glad I could do it almost automatically now. I had some very embarrassing initial conversations with him.

"I thought I could hear voices out here."

The black curtain was pulled back and Lara stood there, watching us with a little smirk on her face. I abruptly turned away from Mason and headed back to the counter.

"Here we go." Lara pushed the bottles towards me.

"Thank you." I opened my purse and dropped them in. "What do I owe you?"

She shook her head. "Don't be silly, this is magic business. You don't owe me anything. In fact, we'll all be thanking you girls once you get rid of that horrid spectre."

She looked over my shoulder. "Hi Mason, I got your text too." She smiled, and Mason walked forward to come and stand behind me.

"Did you find some by any chance?"

"Yes, you're lucky." She reached under the counter and passed him a small packet. "My contact managed to find some at the top of the mountain."

Mason grinned. "Thank you so much, my mother will be delighted."

"My pleasure. You must tell Penny to drop in sometime. I haven't seen her for such a long time."

"Of course. I'm sure she'll call you later once I stop by and give them to her."

Lara nodded. "Also, remind her to keep them in the fridge once opened."

"Herbs for your mum?" I enquired. Mason's mother, Penelope, was a garden witch.

"Yep. She's been after these for the past two months." He held up the sealed packet. It contained some dark purple leaves.

"What does it do?"

"She uses it for some of her healing remedies."

I nodded. "That's where you get your magic touch from."

I blushed as soon as I said those words. *Really? Magic touch?*

Mason did his best to hide his grin and Lara smirked, busing herself with tidying her counter.

"I, um, I should go. I'll let you guys catch up."

My face felt like it was on fire. I backed away, avoiding Mason's eyes.

Just then there was a crash. We spun our heads around to see where the noise came from.

Blaze tottered forward, looking sheepish.

"Blaze?" Mason stepped forward. "What have you done?"

Then I heard the hiss and loud yowl. Atticus. I rushed

past Mason to look for my familiar. He was no longer by the front door, but by the side of the shop, where Lara sold her potion juices.

He was covered in blue juice.

"Atticus," I moved towards him. He shot me a filthy look. "What happened?" I looked around to see if I could spot a towel or some napkins to wipe the juice that was running down his face.

"*Blaze* happened," he spat out.

I turned around, by which time, Lara shoved some napkins into my hand.

"Atticus, I'm so sorry." Blaze said, moving forward, his head bent. "Please, forgive me."

"How about you control that stomach of yours so we wouldn't get into these types of situations in the first place?"

Atticus was fuming, but he allowed me to gently pat him down and to remove as much excess juice as I could.

Mason looked horrified. "My apologies, Atticus. Blaze has a penchant for Lara's blueberry mix. He obviously got too excited."

"You could say that again." Atticus moaned.

"Look, why don't I get you home?" I suggested. "I can give you a nice bath?"

Atticus backed up, all hair on his fur rising. "You will not subject me to that kind of torture."

"It's okay," Lara said. She stepped in front of me and pulled out her wand from the back pocket of her jeans. Then she muttered a few words under her breath and ran her wand over Atticus. A flash of light shot in his direction and then he was back to his full white colour.

"Thank you, Lara," Atticus said, shaking himself out.

I smiled at her and mouthed thank you.

"No bother. You're all clean again, Atticus."

I leaned forward to sniff him. "You smell delicious."

"I'd rather you try not to eat me, thank you."

I looked at Mason and Lara. "We'd better go."

"Atticus? Will you forgive me?" Poor Blaze looked very contrite.

"Don't ever pull a stunt like that again."

"I promise."

"Fine."

I smiled at them and then made my way over to the door. Lara's phone began to ring. "I need to take that, but I'll catch up with you tomorrow, Felicity."

"Sure, thanks again."

Mason walked me out the shop.

"Glad that ended well," he muttered under his breath.

Blaze had remained behind in the shop and sat on the floor.

"He'll be fine." I watched as Atticus tottered ahead, head held high.

"I'm sure it was a bit of a shock. Poor thing. Anyway, before you go, I wanted to ask you something?"

"Sure," I pulled my gaze away from Atticus. "What's up?"

Mason gave me a crooked smile. "I was wondering if you'd like to come to dinner-"

"-Mason," I cut in before I'd have to reject him. "We, er, kind of talked about this. I think it's best we just remain as friends."

And then, before he could say anything further, I dashed off after Atticus.

## CHAPTER FOUR

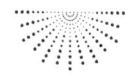

"What was that all about, earlier?"

Atticus was in a much better mood now. After we got back home a little while ago, I dished him out half of my salmon dinner which seemed to appease him.

"What?"

"You know, Mason?"

I sighed. I now regretted running away from him like that. I realised now that I must have come across as very rude. Considering how kind he'd been to me this past month. I dropped my head into my hands. "I think I owe him an apology."

Atticus jumped up onto the sofa next to me. "What for?"

"He asked me out to dinner. I told him no and then ran off after you."

"Very mature." He began to lick his paw.

"Thank you for that. I'm feeling so much better about it now.

Atticus lifted his head. "Well, why don't you just call him, then? That's why you have those mobile phones for, correct?" He then resumed his grooming.

"You want me to call him?"

"Why do humans always have to overcomplicate things? You said you were in the wrong. So, pick up the phone and apologise." Atticus shook his head. "Really, Felicity, for someone so clever and with your talents, you can be rather dim at times."

My mouth dropped open. "No need to be rude."

I picked up my phone from the table and scrolled until I found Mason's number. Then I took a deep breath and hit the call button.

He picked up on the third ring.

"Felicity." He spoke loudly to compensate for the noise in the background. "Hold on, let me go outside where it's quieter."

"Okay." I shouted back.

I waited while he walked away from wherever he was. The noise soon faded.

"Sorry about that," He said.

"No, not at all. I hope I'm not disturbing you."

"It's cool. Just catching up with my friend, Charlie, over a beer. Everything alright?"

I looked over at Atticus who nodded his head.

"I just wanted to say that I'm sorry for walking away from you earlier. I realised it was quite rude."

Mason chuckled. "It's fine. You didn't let me finish. I was asking you to dinner as a friend."

"Oh." I cringed. My heart dropped in embarrassment. I'd read too much into it.

"Don't worry about it. So, would you like to join me?"

"Yes, that would be lovely." I smiled.

"Great - I should mention it will be at my parents' house."

What? *He wants me to come to dinner with his parents? Whoa.* I wasn't sure I was ready for that. What if it meant something to him? I squeezed my eyes shut. Then I felt Atticus's paw on me, and his calming magic seeped into me. I took a deep breath.

"Ok, yes, sure. When?"

"Let me double check with my mother. I'll call you tomorrow if that's alright?"

"That's fine." I smiled weakly. "Thanks, Mason. Bye." Then I hung up the call.

"Meeting the parents already? That's a good sign." Atticus commented and then jumped off the sofa.

I groaned and flopped back on the sofa.

∽

The day started off brighter and the square was bustling with tourists. I was completing some paperwork when my phone began to ring. I grinned when I saw the caller ID.

"Dad!"

"Hello, darling. You alright to talk for a minute?"

"Of course. It's quiet for now. How are you?"

"Not bad, love. Not easy getting back to the grim UK weather."

My dad, George, had arrived back from Spain a week ago. He'd been away since I'd arrived in Agnes and now, I was a completely different person to the one he last saw. Sure, outwardly I was the same, but if only he knew about the dramatic changes I'd experienced in his absence.

"Ugh, I know. Is it raining down in Guildford? It was pouring all day here yesterday, but thankfully brighter this morning."

"Not yet, but the clouds are thick and dark. I expect the rain is on its way over here. Anyway, I won't keep you too long as I know you're busy, but I thought I'd let you know that I've now unpacked and settled, and ready to come to visit you."

"You are? That's fab, Dad. I know you've just got back so I didn't want to hassle you."

"I miss you, love. I can't wait to see you and this village of Agnes, you've decided to settle in. How about I come up on Friday evening - does that work for you?"

Three days away. "Yes, that's perfect. Love you, dad." I missed him terribly.

"You too, Flick. See you then."

I hung up smiling. Dad was the only person in the world who shortened my name. I don't think I could bear for anyone else to call me that - it was our thing.

"Hey, Atticus?" He was hovering about at the back.

"Yes?" He moved into the shop and went to stand at the window, watching the tourists.

"My dad's coming over on Friday. You'll finally get to meet him."

"I'll be charmed, I'm sure. How do you think he'll take the news that his only daughter is in fact, a witch?"

I shook my head. "I've no idea. Perhaps I may decide not to tell him at all. We'll see how it goes. One thing at a time."

"I think you should just tell him. Get it over with."

I chewed my lip. "How's that sound advice working for you?"

He turned around to me and looked at the floor. "You're referring to my feelings for Wilma."

Wilma was a beautiful black familiar cat, who lived in the next town of Lawnes. Atticus had deep feelings for her.

"Well, have you told her how you feel?"

"No?" He lifted his big blue eyes to me.

"Hmmm…maybe you should take some of your own advice since you're so good at dishing it out."

"It's complicated."

"Oh so, it's okay for things to be complicated for you, but not me?"

"Please, Felicity. I'm not in the mood for your petulance."

And with that, he strolled back to where he came from. Probably my bed.

∼

Since it was quiet for most of the day, I had a chance to call a couple of my suppliers to enquire about the aventurine stone for Lara's engagement ring. Plus, I finalised my ideas and was ready to present three different variations to Luca. Once that was done, I worked on the necklace for Mia. That was a lot easier since I knew she favoured simple designs. I located a beautiful heart-shaped rose quartz stone and placed an order for it. Mia's bracelet was sterling silver I matched it with a delicate ball chain necklace. Afterwards, I called Luca to tell him I was ready with some ideas. He was busy for the next day or so but promised to pop in to talk them over with me.

Luca Rossini was a bigshot businessman. I wasn't exactly sure what he did, but I think it had something to do with property management. Either way, from what I'd heard, he was loaded and lived in an opulent home in Lawnes. Which is another reason I was so grateful to him for giving me a chance to design Lara's ring instead of going to a top-end jeweller.

After I closed the shop, I headed back upstairs to the flat. It was raining again and all I really wanted was an early dinner and my book.

A while later, I was just warming up my microwave meal, when Mason rang.

"Hi," I said.

"Felicity, can you please make it stop?"

"The rain?"

"Yes. Can you tap into those special elemental powers of yours and turn off the tap?"

I laughed. "I'll work on that."

He paused. "So, what are you up to?"

I glanced down at my slippered feet and my towelling robe.

"Well, I'm living the high life. Let's see. I had only three customers today, so the day totally dragged. I've just had a nice bath and I can't wait to read the next chapter of my book. Oh, and I'm warming up a microwave meal."

"Yikes. That bad, huh?"

I grinned. "Thanks. You know just how to make a girl feel special."

Mason hesitated. I could almost feel something was on the tip of his tongue. My mind wandered off. How *did* he treat his girlfriends? I bet he was an amazing boyfriend.

"I guess you'll never know." His voice was husky, though his voice was teasing.

I groaned loudly. "Mason! Stop listening in on my thoughts."

"I can't help it." He laughed. "Besides, I've shown you how to block them."

"But I keep forgetting," I protested. "You're the only one who has this connection to me."

He cleared his throat. We were going down a road that I didn't want to face. "So, about plans for dinner."

"Oh, yes."

"Does Thursday night suit you?"

"Yes, that's fine. My dad, George, is coming up on Friday."

"That's great, Felicity. I'm sure you can't wait."

"I can't, it's the longest I've ever gone without seeing him. But Thursday is great, thank you. Can I bring anything?"

"No, just your lovely self." he replied. "I'll pick you up at seven."

"Wait, do you own a car?"

He laughed. "Just the Harley." Then his voice grew serious. "I promise, you'll be fine. I'd never let anything bad happen to you."

My stomach did that thing again where it felt like a swarm of butterflies had taken flight. But the microwave beeped, and our temporary spell was broken.

"Thank you, I'll see you Thursday." I said softy.

CHAPTER FIVE

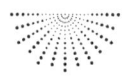

"Felicity, come on through."

I smiled at Desmond and followed him through the police station and to his office at the back.

"Thanks for seeing me," I said, pulling out a seat opposite him.

"No problem. So, tell me again, how I can help you?"

"I wanted to ask you a favour and I'm hoping you'd be agreeable."

A small smile pulled at the corners of Desmond's mouth. He linked his hands together on his desk and pushed his chair forward. "I think we all know around here just how persuasive you can be."

I dipped my head and smiled. Somehow, I'd been able to piece together clues and helped to solve the last two murders. I felt like Desmond finally respected me.

"Well, in that case, I'll cut to the chase. I was wondering if you have any files on The River Inn?"

He frowned. "Well, I've been in Agnes for most of my life and I've only ever known the place as a B&B. However, were you aware that Edmund's father, who is mostly retired these days, headed up this area when he was actively chief constable?"

Edmund Townsend owned Town's End Garage. He'd helped me with my car when I first arrived in Agnes. "I had no idea," I said.

"Well, as I said, he's supposed to be retired, but he likes to keep abreast of crime matters in our village. I still send him a monthly report."

"I see. Well, do you think he'd know about the history of The River Inn, then?'

"I should think so. He's what, approaching eighty now? Still sharp as they come. In fact, maybe I can look it up myself." He pulled his computer towards him and then paused. "Actually, why do you want to know?" His eyes narrowed. "What are you up to, Felicity?"

*Oh, you know. Just trying to banish a malevolent spirit later tonight.* "Nothing, I just wanted to find out about the history," I lied with a sweet smile.

Desmond shook his head and tapped on the keys. "You're not a good liar, by the way. But I'll give you the benefit of the doubt."

My face heated but I didn't say anything while he tapped on his keys. Then he stopped and stared at the screen.

"Ah, here we are."

"Anything interesting?"

"Yes. Apparently, back in the '60s, The River Inn looked like it used to be a mental institution." He peered closer at the screen. "We have a few files on the place so something must have happened there."

"Desmond, I know it's classified information, but would you let me have a quick peek at the files?"

He sat back in his chair and studied my face. "First you need to be truthful. Why do you want to know?"

I sighed. I couldn't tell him about the spectre, but I wanted to be as honest as I could.

"Becky Scarborough has left to go to London. She told me she thinks the place is haunted."

Desmond scoffed. "Ah, yes, she sprouted the same nonsense to me. So, what, you think the same now?'

I shrugged noncommittally. "I've no idea but I thought that maybe if I looked into the history, we could convince her to come back? I know she's lived here most of her life too, and it's a shame she feels this way."

"As far as I'm concerned, that place just need an update and a good lick of paint. She can't blame her lack of customers on some so-called spirit." He laughed and shook his head. "But okay, if it makes you happy, I'll dig out the files from the back. It'll be in the archives section, so you'll have to give me a few minutes." He stood up from his chair.

"Thank you, Desmond, I really appreciate it."

He nodded and then disappeared out of the room.

My phone beeped with a WhatsApp message from our group chat, with Mia, Darcey and Emma. It was Mia.

*Have you got anything?*

*Not, yet, but Desmond's getting the files now.*

*Good work. May come in handy depending on what we see later tonight. Still ok for 10.30 meet-up?*

*Yes. See you in a bit.*

I glanced around Desmond's office while I waited. It didn't surprise me that it was neat and tidy, with everything in an ordered fashion. I couldn't imagine him being messy.

Footsteps sounded from behind me, and I turned around in my chair. Desmond stood there holding a slim, aged brown folder.

"This is all we've got on *The River Inn*. I can't locate the other two right now." He passed it across to me.

"Thank you." I stood up from my chair.

"You can use one of the interview rooms. But I need to leave in thirty minutes, hopefully that will give you enough time."

I took the file and made my way out of his office.

Once inside the interview room, I shut the door and pulled out the plastic chair. Then I opened the file. A few dust motes scattered in the air and I blew them away as I pulled out the paperwork. Like Desmond said, it used to be a mental institution for men. There were a few reports of stabbings inside the home, which resulted in a couple of deaths. Another report of a suicide where the patient jumped off the building. Then more paperwork which consisted of interviews with key staff members following the incidents. I looked to see if I recognised any staff name, but they were all strangers. There was one more report of a patient who was accused of murdering two women in the area, but as I looked through it, it seemed there wasn't enough evidence to convict him. Other than that, there wasn't anything else that stood out to me. I put all the paperwork back together and slipped them back into the file. I was hoping to find a connection with the spectre and a patient, but nothing seemed to link together. I suppose it was worth a try.

"Are you quite sure I can't come with you?" Atticus enquired later that night as I got ready to leave to meet the girls.

I shook my head, despite his many protests. "No, Atticus. It's not safe and I'd hate to see you injured again. I couldn't bear it." I shuddered at the memory of Raphael flinging Atticus across the room and rendering him unconscious.

"Okay, I won't come in but I'll be standing outside The River Inn just in case." He looked at me with a stubborn glare and I knew it would be no use arguing.

"Fine."

"Fine."

I gathered my wand and the extra tourmaline crystals I'd brought for us to use. I had used it the time before when Lara and I had first encountered the spirit. Since the stone helped to protect us from negative energy, the ghost didn't approve of it one bit.

"Okay, I'm ready." I took a deep breath and slipped my wand into my pocket. "Let's go."

We left the flat and made our way across the square in the direction of *The River Inn* which was less than a ten-minute walk away. Atticus moved quietly besides me, both of us deep in thought. At least it hadn't rained today so the ground wasn't wet for Atticus' paws.

As we neared The River Inn, I instinctively looked up at the window from where the ghost had thrown Lara from. It was still broken, but there wasn't any sign of movement from what I could see from down here. I looked towards the entrance and saw three shadows waiting by the bush. As I moved closer, Darcey, Emma and Mia stepped out, along with their familiars. Three black cats who were also siblings.

"At least you'll have some company while you wait out here," I muttered to Atticus.

I came to a stand in front of my friends.

"Ready?" Emma enquired.

I nodded and reached into my jacket pocket. "Here." I passed around the tourmaline stones to all three of them.

"Thanks," Mia said, glancing up at the building. "How about we banish this ghost once and for all?"

"Let's do it," Darcey said, stepping forward.

"Wait," Emma said, holding onto her arm. "Nothing foolish, okay? We don't know how dangerous this thing is. Lara made me promise to leave if things get out of hand."

I exhaled. "Got it." I looked down at Atticus who had joined the other familiars. All four of them looked at us expectantly.

"We'll be fine," I assured them, sounding braver than I felt. Then I walked up to the door, with Emma in the lead. I glanced around but thankfully no one was about at this time of night. Emma muttered a few words and the front door clicked. She turned the handle and then we all stepped inside.

Mia was the last one in and gagged. "What in all the Nature's name is that stench?"

We simultaneously threw our arms across our nose, with bile rising at the back of my throat.

"Well, that's not a very pleasant welcome, is it?" Emma moved forward towards the stairs, with a look of determination. She wore a cross body bag which held the containment jar imbued with the spell to capture the spectre.

I took a deep breath and removed my arm, following behind her.

CHAPTER SIX

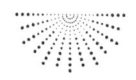

The stairs were creaky as we quietly made our way up to the next floor. Darcey was behind me and Mia brought up the rear. All four of us had our wands out in preparation, their tips casting a glow of light for us, to lead the way.

We reached the first floor and I peered around into the open bedrooms. My jaw dropped open in disbelief.

"Oh, my stars. It's really done a number on this place."

The girls piled into the bedroom, pointing their wands on the wall. The last time I was here, the spirit had attached itself to the top floor, but now it looked like it was everywhere. The walls were covered in black mould, which absolutely stank. Darcey began to gag and stepped out the room. We all did the same.

I looked around and peered into the other three bedrooms. Again, all the walls were damaged.

"I can't feel anything here on this floor, can you?" I whispered to the girls.

Emma shook her head, looking upstairs. A mist had begun to swirl at the top of the stairs.

"It knows we're here," I said quietly. "Brace yourselves."

This time, I moved forward to the stairs leading up to the top floor. Again, like the last time, the temperature dropped as soon as I stood on them. Luckily, I had warned the others and we were dressed in appropriately in warm layers.

I crept up the stairs as quietly as I could, with Emma, Darcey and Mia right behind me. The further up we got, the colder the air. Then we reached the top stair. I turned to my friends. In the glow of the light coming from our wands, I could see their noses were bright red, as were their cheeks. I'm sure I reflected the same appearance. It was freezing up here.

"I'm going to push the door open."

"Don't use your hand," Emma warned. "Remember Lara got an ice burn the last time?"

I nodded. I held my wand at the door and a shot of magic blasted through my wand. A bright blue spark flew out and made contact with the door, slamming it open.

Before we could prepare ourselves, the mist

surrounded us and engulfed us like a thick fog. I couldn't see out of it. It was forcing itself into my mouth and I struggled not to swallow. I couldn't properly breathe, and panic rose in my chest as I fumbled for my wand.

A deep roar of laughter came from the room, but then I felt Emma next to me and the mist evaporated. We stumbled forward.

"Nice one," I whispered to her, regaining my breath.

"You're a meanie, aren't you?" Emma said with a clear and loud voice. "But you've outstayed your welcome, so it's time to go."

"I'm not going anywhere, you stupid witch."

The spectre was on the wall by the window, a thick black curtain of smoke with glowing red eyes. As we watched, it extracted itself and came at us with force. We fell backwards as it punched its way through us. It felt like shards of ice piercing through me. Mia fell to the ground and as soon as I regained my footing, I rushed over to her.

"Are you okay?" I asked, helping her up.

She coughed and nodded. "I wasn't expecting that."

The ghost swirled around us, laughing and growling, shifting into patterns of the figure of eight.

"On the count of three," I said. We spun around the room to see where it had gone. It was in the bathroom and was heading our way again for another round.

I grabbed Emma's hand, who took Darcey's and then

Mia's. We joined ourselves together just in time and I felt a bolt of electricity shoot up my arm. Sparks shot out from our arms as our magic linked. Then with our free hand, I counted to three and we aimed the tourmaline at the spectre.

It screamed and growled in pain, and then slowly, it fell to the ground, withering on the floor.

"Oh boy, you don't like that, do you?" I said, stepping forward. "Quick, Emma."

Emma reached into her bag with lightning speed and opened the jar, filled with the magic oil and herbs. Then we joined hands once again and chanted the words to the spell. As we watched, the black mist roared and screeched but was drawn into the jar like a magnet.

"I think we got it." Mia said, slamming the lid onto it and screwing it tightly closed. Inside, the mist threw itself against the jar in a rage, howling, but it was muted from the outside.

"Let's get it out of here," Emma said, reaching for the jar. She winced.

"Are you okay?" I asked, stepping forward.

"Yeah, it's just really cold." She shook her hand out.

I quickly reached into her bag and handed her the blanket.

"Take this, it will help to keep it off your hands."

She wrapped the jar in the blanket and then stuffed it into her bag.

"Good work, team." Darcey said, glancing around at the walls. "Just checking that we've got all of it."

Mia walked across the room, pointing her wand to do a final sweep. By now, all of us were beyond freezing and my teeth had begun to chatter.

"Yep, it's done," she declared. "Let's go."

We dashed out of the room and back down the stairs and out into the open. Then we all bent over to take lungfuls of clean air.

"What are you going to do with it?" I asked Emma once we had regained our breath.

"I think I'll bury it, deep in the forest."

I hugged each one of them in turn.

"Be careful." I said as I watched them walk towards Emma's car.

∽

"Are you okay?" Atticus asked once we were back inside our flat. "You're not looking too good."

"I feel quite nauseous," I replied, heading for the bathroom.

"Oh no, perhaps I should make myself scarce? I don't think I can take another episode of you retching."

"It was only the once, Atticus. And that was when I first used a real spell back at Lottie's B&B."

He shuddered. "But the memory is etched forever. These things don't just go away."

I ignored him and splashed my face. I was exhausted and I just really needed to sleep.

I managed to brush my teeth and then I crawled onto the top of the covers on my bed. I didn't even have the energy to get undressed.

Despite his teasing, Atticus must have passed some magic to me. I felt him on the bed next to me and soon after, the sickness began to fade.

"Thank you," I whispered before I fell asleep.

It must have been a couple hours or so later when I felt Atticus pawing my face. I couldn't bring myself to open my eyes. I also realised I was freezing cold. I began to shiver uncontrollably.

"Felicity. Wake up."

I curled up into a ball. "Please, let me sleep…"

"You're burning up with a fever, please wake up."

I couldn't. All I wanted was to fall back into the deep sleep. But I was so cold, and I couldn't stop shaking. I tried my hardest to stop and go back to my dreamless state.

Why was someone shaking me? Was I dreaming?

"Felicity? Sweetheart, you need to wake up."

*Mason?* Why was Mason calling me from my dream?

The gentle shaking on my shoulder continued. I tried to move away, but I had no energy. Finally, I managed to open an eyelid.

"Mason? Am I dreaming?"

Mason's face was inches from mine. I could just about make out his features from the moonlight coming in through my window, where I hadn't drawn the curtains.

"No, you're not dreaming. I'm here, and so is Blaze. Atticus signalled for me. You're extremely sick. I need you drink this, okay? I'm going to help you sit up, now."

I began to shiver again, and Mason grabbed the blanket from the end of my bed and wrapped it across my shoulders as he helped me to sit up. My entire body felt like lead. Atticus snuggled up next to me and I appreciated the warmth from his fur.

"What time is it?" I mumbled.

"It's after one in the morning."

I sucked in a breath. What was he doing here so late?

"Why are you here? I'm fine?'

I caught the look of concern that Atticus shared with Mason. I scrubbed at my eyes, but my energy was going again.

"You've got a very high fever." He reached for a cup by

my bedside. It smelt of herbs. "I need to you drink this, Sweetheart. Please. It will make you better."

I tried to reach my hand for the cup, but I couldn't muster the strength. Mason moved closer to my side, held the back of my head and then gently brought the cup to my lips. I took a tentative sip of the warm liquid. It tasted a little like green tea but with a combination of some other herbs I couldn't place. I took a couple more sips and then pulled back to catch my breath.

"What is this?" I asked.

"It's one of my mother's remedies. I'm afraid the black magic from the spirit earlier has affected you badly."

My first thought was about my friends.

"They're fine," he answered.

"Why did I have such a reaction, then?"

He frowned as he once again brought the cup to my lips. I took a few more sips and managed to drain the cup.

"I'm not entirely sure…but let's not worry about it for now. I just need to get you well again."

"Thank you." I tried to smile but even the muscles in my mouth ached.

"Let's get you into bed," Mason said, taking charge. "Do you have something more comfortable to sleep in? Your clothes are damp from your fever."

I nodded and pointed to the cupboard. "Second drawer down. There are pyjamas in there."

Mason moved across the room and a few seconds later, he returned with a fresh pair.

"Thank you."

"Do you need help?" He asked.

I shook my head. "I'll be okay. Just give me a few minutes."

"I'll be right outside. Come on, guys."

Atticus, Blaze and Mason made their way out of the room. The remedy was starting to work as I was beginning to feel better. I managed to change and pulled out the covers from my bed, then I slipped inside.

A wave of tiredness came over me. I was just about to tell Mason I was done but, suddenly, I couldn't keep my eyes open. I was pulled back down into a deep slumber.

CHAPTER SEVEN

I woke up before the light. I turned to my bedside table and the clock told me it was just after six am.

For a moment I wondered if I'd dreamt about Mason and Blaze being here last night. I sat up in bed and I felt absolutely fine. Whatever happened to me last night had thankfully passed. I couldn't believe how unwell I had felt.

Atticus was sleeping on the end of the bed. He slit open an eye and padded over to me, purring loudly.

"The patient is awake. How are you feeling?"

"Much better, thank you." I stroked him and dropped a kiss on his forehead. "Atticus, was Mason here or did I dream that?"

"I hadn't realised you had regular dreams about him."

I smirked. "Very funny."

"He's sleeping on the couch with Blaze in the living room."

"He stayed over?" My hands automatically went to my hair to smooth down the knots that resembled a bird's nest at the back of my head.

"He didn't want to leave your side. You were very unwell, Felicity, and you gave me quite a fright. As you wouldn't wake up, I didn't know what to do. I sent a message to Blaze who alerted Mason. They teleported here within minutes of my message."

I exhaled deeply. It felt like Mason was always coming to my rescue. No matter what, in the short time I'd known him, he was always there for me.

I swung my legs out of the bed and onto the carpet. "I'll just take a peek at them. If they're still asleep, I'm going to grab a shower."

"I would if I were you."

"Not funny, Atticus." I cringed at the memory of how sweaty I was last night from the fever.

I tiptoed into the hallway and then stepped into the front room. Mason was fast asleep on the sofa. He didn't look particularly comfortable with his tall frame curled up like that. I felt a stab of guilt. Blaze was on the floor by him but as soon as he saw me, he stood up and trotted over to me, tail wagging.

"Morning," I whispered, and bent down and scratched behind his ear. I placed my finger to my lips. "Let Mason sleep, I'm going to take a quick shower." I kissed his head. "Thank you for looking after me last night."

Blaze followed me back into the bedroom. Atticus had resumed his position at the end of the bed and Blaze looked up at me with big brown eyes. I was going to change the sheets anyway.

I smiled. "Go on then, you can get up on the bed too."

He wagged his tail and jumped up onto the bed, spinning around a couple of times, before he found a comfortable spot. "Thank you, this is better than the floor," he said. Then he lowered his head onto his paws and closed his eyes.

I grabbed some clean clothes and walked into the bathroom. The hot spray of the shower washed away the last of my illness and I felt invigorated by the time I finished. Although I may have stayed in a little longer than anticipated as the bathroom was filled with steam by the time I was done. I brushed out my damp hair, applied my usual amount of light make-up and then opened the door.

I was immediately greeted with the smell of eggs.

"Mason?"

I padded into the kitchen and saw Mason standing over the hob, frying some eggs. He turned around as I approached, and my breath caught in my chest. His hair was all over the place, but oh my stars, the man was still ridiculously handsome. Did I also mention that he was only wearing his vest, which showed off his toned biceps, the dark inking that covered one arm, and the outline of his abs?

"Good morning, you look great." He said, putting down the spatula. He flipped the eggs onto a plate. "I take it you're feeling okay now?"

I smiled, feeling shy. "Yes, I'm back to normal." I walked over to him. "Mason, about last night, thank you for coming over and bringing the remedy. I didn't realise how sick I was."

He put the plate down on the counter and his bright blue eyes bore into mine with an intensity I'd never experienced before. I couldn't tear my eyes away even if I tried.

"I was so worried about you." He frowned. "Felicity, I wasn't comfortable about the four of your tackling that spirit. I knew I should have said something to Lara."

I shook my head. "No, it wasn't your fault. Besides, I wanted to help. And we did it, we got the evil thing."

"But at what cost to you? I can't bear to see you suffer like that."

I blinked and lowered my eyes. "I would have been fine."

"Yes, you would have because you're an amazing witch,

but you need to learn some more protection spells to guard yourself before you tackle this kind of thing again. Were you wearing your necklace?"

I pressed my lips together. "I rarely take it off, but I polished it last night. I guess I forgot to put it back on. But Darcey, Emma and Mia are fine, right?"

"Yes, but they've been witches all their lives," he said softly. "That kind of thing is natural for them."

I smiled and tucked my damp hair behind my ears. "Got it. I'll go put it back on; give me a sec." I rushed back into my bedroom and saw my necklace on the cloth where I'd left it to dry on my bedside table, yesterday evening. I slipped it back on and an immediate sense of calm fell over me. Then I went back to the kitchen. Mason noticed it and smiled, as he buttered the second piece of toast.

"Come on, let's have breakfast. Are you hungry? I've already fed Atticus and Blaze."

I glanced over to them. They were both sitting on the floor, looking content with Atticus grooming his paws. "Thank you. But what did Blaze eat?"

"Atticus kindly shared his roast chicken."

I grinned. "Well, that's a first."

Breakfast was delicious. Whatever energy I had lacking was replenished after Mason's delicious food.

"Thank you, that was amazing. You can cook for me anytime," I joked.

"My pleasure. And for the record, I wouldn't mind making you breakfast every day." He winked and I ducked my head biting back my smile. Mason stood to gather our plates. I carried over our cups to the sink.

"Please, you've done enough," I said, stopping him from his attempt to wash up.

"Okay, I guess I'd better head home. So, what are your plans for today? Are you still okay for dinner later?"

"Definitely. I'll be in the shop as usual. And you?"

I knew Mason was self-employed. He did something along the lines of online trading.

He shrugged, draining his orange juice. "I need to meet a client later, but that's about it. A pretty chilled day ahead. I'll pick you up at seven."

Then he bent his head and dropped a soft kiss on my cheek. "I'm glad you're ok."

～

Luca stepped into the shop later that afternoon.

"Hi," I greeted, smiling as he approached my counter. "Thanks for coming all this way."

He blew some warm air into his hands. "Don't be silly,

I should be thanking you." Then he unzipped his leather flying jacket and took a seat at the stool.

I pulled out my sketchbook and we spent some time going through my final designs. As soon as he saw the second drawing, he pointed at the ring.

"That's the style I had in mind." He looked up at me and grinned. "It's perfect."

"Do you want to see the other one I drew?"

"Sure, but I already know she'll love this one."

Next, I explained to him the meaning of the crystal I intended to use, and he seemed equally happy with it.

"I was thinking to set the stone in eighteen carat gold; however, I was wondering if you would like to add some little diamonds on the shoulder of ring?"

Again, I pulled out a separate drawing to show him what I meant. I kind of thought Lara might appreciate the extra sparkle.

Luca liked the idea very much.

"I don't normally deal with diamonds, but I know of one supplier who ethically sources these stones."

"That sounds perfect. How soon do you think you'll be able to make it?"

I smiled. "My supplier is on standby. I was just waiting for the green light from you, so I'll now go ahead and order the stones and gold. I could have it ready for you by this time next week, all being well? In plenty of time for Valentine's Day."

Luca smiled and stood up from the stool. "You're a gem yourself, Felicity. I can't wait to see the real thing."

Then like the true Italian gent he was, he leaned over and kissed both my cheeks. "Grazie. Ciao, Bella."

I waved him off, thrilled that he loved my design. I also couldn't wait for the big announcement.

After I closed my shop, I replied to yet another group message from Emma, Darcey and Mia, who had continued to send me messages throughout the day, checking up on me. Earlier I'd made Mason and the girls promise me that they wouldn't tell Lara. Reluctantly, they all agreed. I knew Lara would have felt terrible, but it was my fault for not wearing my necklace. Plus, I really needed to work on my protection spell work.

Then I went back upstairs to my flat. Atticus followed me as he'd just come back from a walk.

"How's Wilma?" I enquired, as we sat on the sofa together. I'd need to start getting ready soon, but I had a bit of time.

"She's fine," Atticus replied. "I think I'm almost ready to reveal my feelings to her."

I reached over and stroked him. "That's great. What do you think she'll say?"

"I'm not privy to the modern female mind. Living with you is complicated enough."

Then he jumped off the sofa and wondered off. What had gotten into him?

It was almost seven. I gave myself one final look in the mirror. While I didn't want to overdress, I also wanted to make a good impression. A dress was out since I was going on the back of Mason's Harley, so I selected a plain black jumpsuit. I tucked my necklace underneath and selected a long beaded, turquoise necklace, with matching stud earrings. My makeup was smoky around my eyes and I went for a light pink lip. Then I selected some heeled boots and grabbed my small clutch. I finished off with a light spritz of my favourite floral perfume and glanced at the clock. It just turned seven and at the same time, the buzzer sounded to my flat. I glanced out the window and saw Mason standing there. He waved up at me.

*Oh boy, here we go.*

"Atticus, I'm leaving now."

He was snoozing behind the sofa. "Have fun," he groggily replied.

I grabbed my thick, padded jacket and headed down the stairs. Then I opened the front door. Mason greeted me with a warm smile. He was wearing his leather jacket but had on some smarter, chino style, trousers.

"Wow." He low-whistled, raking his eyes over me.

"Stop it." I shook my head, but I smiled.

"Sorry," Mason exhaled, and turned his attention to the Harley. "So, you've never ridden on a bike, before, right?"

I shook my head, nervously eyeing up the steel machine parked next to him.

"I promise, you're going to love it."

CHAPTER EIGHT

*A*s we cruised along the road towards Oxford, I could see why Mason loved his bike. Riding with the wind in your face, coupled with the comfort of the Harley and the freedom of the open road, was something I knew I could get used to. After my initial nerves when we took off, I soon relaxed. It felt amazing and I knew I was hooked. Mason kept checking on me every few minutes over his shoulder to make sure I was okay.

"So, do you hate it?" He shouted.

I leaned further into his back. "Are you serious? I love it!"

Mason tipped his head back and laughed. "I knew you would. Are you holding on tight?"

"Yes, stop worrying," I replied. Truth was, I was

enjoying the feel of my wrapped arms around Mason Reed a little too much.

All too soon we entered Oxford and then headed out to a residential area, where the houses were larger and further spaced out. Mason pointed to a house in front of us and leaned his head back.

"That's my parents' house up ahead."

There was no turning back now. The house was a huge, detached mansion. On either side of the front door were two spiral shaped topiary trees, which were lit up with clear fairy lights. I took a deep breath as Mason pulled the Harley into the drive. I looked to my right and saw a couple of expensive looking cars parked by the garage.

Mason killed the engine, and I lowered my hands from his waist. Then he kicked out the stand and stepped over the bike offering me his hand as I also reluctantly got off.

"Thanks, that was amazing." I fiddled with the clip on my helmet and finally managed to unlock then. Then I slipped it off my head. I dreaded to think of the state of my hair. Mason reached over and smoothed down a lock by my ear.

"You didn't warn me about helmet hair," I joked, doing my best to smooth it out.

"You still look amazing. Are you ready to meet my family?"

I forced a smile on my face and Mason burst out laughing. "I promise, they're good people. Come on." He reached out his hand to me and I automatically slipped mine into his without thinking. Then we stood at the door and Mason pressed the bell. I untangled my hand from his and looked straight ahead to avoid his gaze.

The door flew open and a petite lady, with a sharp blonde bob and twinkling blue eyes, smiled at us. I could see who Mason inherited his stunning aqua eyes from. She exuded elegance and wore cream palazzo trousers with a light blue shirt, tucked into the waistband.

"Mason, you're on time for once." Her eyes landed on me. "And this lovely young lady must be Felicity." She reached both of her hands out to me and took mine into hers. "Welcome."

"Thank you, Mrs Reed, it's a pleasure to meet you."

"Please, you'll remind me of my mother-in-law. Penny's fine." She pulled me into a hug, and I immediately felt comfortable. Penny had this safe and calming aura about her that settled my nerves. I couldn't describe it, but it felt kind and strong, an earthy presence that just made you want to relax. Finally, she pulled away. I smiled and glanced up at Mason who was looking as us curiously.

"Come on through." She looked at Mason. "Your father and great grandfather are in the study. Will you pry them apart, Mason, and tell them to join us in the dining room?"

"Sure."

"Don't worry about Felicity, we'll be just fine." She motioned for me to follow her. "Come on, you can help me with the drinks."

"Of course."

"Mason, be a gentleman and take her coat."

"I was just about to do that, Mother." He rolled his eyes at me.

"I can see that." She commented.

I grinned, quickly retrieved my clutch from the inside pocket of my jacket and then shrugged it off. I handed my jacket to Mason and then followed Penny's clicking kitten heels on the tiled hallway to the back of the house.

"You have a beautiful home," I commented, glancing around.

"Thank you, dear. It's been a long work in progress, but I think I finally have it the way I want."

We entered the kitchen, which was huge with pristine white cupboards, and black marble counter tops. A huge island occupied the middle, on which stood a vase full of long-stemmed cream roses. I could smell their divine perfume even from where I stood.

The tiled floor was off white. It was a stunning designer kitchen.

"Take a seat at the island, I'm just going to grab the drinks from the fridge."

"Thank you." I walked over to the stool and perched on the edge. Then I opened my clutch and pulled out the small cream gift box.

Penny came over with a jug of what looked like melon juice.

"A little something to say thank you for welcoming me into your home." I smiled at the look of surprise on her face as I pushed my gift across to her.

"Felicity? You didn't have to get me anything." She placed the jug down and took the box into her hands.

"I wanted to. Actually, I made it; I hope you like it."

I watched as Penny pulled apart the green bow. Then she opened the box and her eyes widened in surprise. She carefully took out the necklace and held it up in front of her. It sparkled where it caught the light from the overhead spotlights.

"Felicity, this is absolutely beautiful. Thank you."

"You're most welcome." I grinned.

Earlier today, while the shop was quiet, I'd made Penny a delicate silver monstera leaf pendant. I'd also worked in some tiny fluorite polished crystals which ran down the centre of the leaf.

Penny opened the clasp and slipped on the necklace, adjusting the collar of her shirt. "How do I look?"

"Lovely. It suits you."

She walked around the island and thanked me again with a kiss on my cheeks.

Then we poured the juice into the glasses.

"What is this?" I sniffed my glass.

"It's cloudberry with a little magic." She winked. "Try it."

I took a sip. It tasted a little like raspberry, but I also got a little kick of something else. "Is it alcohol?"

She shook her head. "It isn't, but it will still give you a little buzz."

"In that case, I'd better go easy," I laughed.

"Come on, let's go through. It's time to eat."

I helped her collect the other glasses and trailed behind her as she led us into the dining room, which was off to the right of the kitchen, through an arc.

As soon as we entered the dining room, I saw a huge oak table, which was intricately covered with carvings. It was twelve-seater but only five places were set for tonight. A beautiful crystal chandelier hung over the middle of the room, casting a soft glow over the table. My eyes landed on a huge painting which was on the wall behind the head of the table, at the other end of the room. Penny must have caught my line of vision.

"Ah, those are the Reed men in the family. Randall got it done last year."

I placed the glasses onto the table and walked over the thick pile carpet to the painting. I hadn't met Mason's father, Randall yet, but besides the eye colour, Mason looked like a younger version of him. I concentrated on Mason's picture. He wore a small smile and had on a smart shirt and a pair of jeans.

Penny came to stand next to me. "He flat out refused to wear smart trousers."

I smiled at that. Mason was a bit of a rebel at heart. Penny pointed out the rest of the men.

"So, as you've probably guessed, that's Randall, who you'll meet in a moment. Next to Randall is Michael, Mason's grandfather. He's in the Cayman Islands at present, which is where he prefers to spend his winters. And then, besides Michael, is Quentin, Mason's great-grandfather."

I nodded, looking at all of them in turn. Randall and Michael still looked relatively young, but Quentin had a shock of white hair, which he backcombed. His green eyes bore into me as I stared at the painting. I could feel the strength of his power even before meeting him.

We heard footsteps approaching and I turned around, ready to greet them. Mason came into the dining room first and came to stand by me.

"Everything okay so far?" He asked quietly.

"Absolutely." I smiled back up at him.

Next was Randall and behind him, Quentin. Mason stepped forward. "G.G and Father, I'd like you both to meet Felicity."

Randall, like Penny, immediately made me feel at ease. He extended his hand with a warm smile on his face, his eyes crinkling at the corners. "Welcome to our home, Felicity. We've heard so much about you." Then he pulled me in and kissed both my cheeks.

"Thank you, Mr. Reed."

He clasped my hand into his. "You must call me, Randall."

"Thank you. Randall it is."

I peered over his shoulder to find Quentin watching me closely with narrowed eyes.

Oh, my stars. He did not look impressed at all.

CHAPTER NINE

"Great-grandfather, please meet, Felicity." Mason said, coming to stand next to me. He turned to me. "I call him G.G as you may have gathered."

I extended my hand. "It's lovely to meet you, Sir."

"Hmmm." He glanced at my hand and then back at me. The look he gave me sent a shiver up my spine. Then he ignored my outstretched hand and proceeded to the table. I dropped my hand, my face burning with embarrassment.

Randall shot me an apologetic look, whereas Mason just looked plain confused.

Penny cleared her throat. "Let's eat, shall we?"

I swallowed and took a seat next to Mason. Underneath the table he reached for my hand and gave me a quick squeeze. I smiled weakly at him. I'd no idea what I'd done to offend Quentin Reed.

Penny picked up a little silver bell and shook it. To my surprise, moments later, plates flew in from the kitchen. One of them landed perfectly in front of me.

"That's amazing," I whispered to Mason.

"Gazpacho, I hope you'll enjoy it." Penny said and picked up her spoon. We all followed suit.

The cold soup was absolutely divine. "This is delicious," I said to Penny, taking another appreciative mouthful.

"Thank you," She replied beaming. "Tomatoes and herbs from my little garden."

Mason snorted. "Mother, I'd hardly refer to the garden as *little*." He turned to me. "I'll have to give you a tour some other time."

"That's if she's welcome back," Quentin muttered. He tried to say it quietly, but we all heard him, nonetheless.

"Father, please." Randall's tone was firm. Then he turned to me with an apologetic look. "How are you settling into Agnes?"

I placed my spoon down. Despite the delicious soup, I'd almost lost my appetite with that last comment. It was clear I wasn't welcome here according to Quentin. "I love it so far." I replied, feebly. "Everyone's made me feel very welcome." I stuffed a piece bread into my mouth. *Except you, old man.*

"Have you heard from your mother?" Quentin asked from where he was sitting diagonally opposite me.

"My mother died when I was a toddler."

"I wasn't referring to her," he snapped.

I gave him a blank stare.

"G.G…"

"Don't interrupt me, Mason. I'm speaking to the girl."

I inhaled deeply. An uncomfortable silence fell over the table. Penny clapped her hands.

"Quentin, what on earth has got into you? This is no way to treat our guest."

Quentin's eyes flashed at Penny. "In that case, I won't be staying for the main course." He picked up his napkin, dabbed his mouth at the corners and flung it back down. He roughly pushed back his chair and glared at me.

"I don't like you, girl. You have the scent of the fae on you." With that, he stormed out the door. Silence. None of us said anything until Randall pushed back his chair and followed after his grandfather.

"I'm so sorry." Mason's voice was anguished.

My face was on fire from the shame and embarrassment of how I was spoken to. How dare Quentin Reed insult me like that? I placed my napkin on the table and turned to Penny with a forced smile on my face.

"Penny, thank you very much for having me over, but I think it's best I leave."

She looked just as distressed as I pushed back my chair to stand. "Felicity, I'm so sorry. But you don't have to leave. This is my home and you're very welcome here.

"Thank you. But perhaps we'll try another time. If you don't mind, I would like to go home."

She furrowed her brows and nodded resignedly. "You're welcome back anytime."

Mason rose up from his seat next to me, but I shook my head at him.

"Please, stay and finish dinner. I'll get a taxi back home."

"I'm walking you out."

I nodded at Penny and followed Mason, hoping that I wouldn't see Quentin on my way. Thankfully as we walked in silence to the front door, they weren't to be seen.

"They're in the study again." Mason said, pulling open a cupboard by the front door and taking out my coat. I took it from him and slipped it on.

"Felicity." Mason ran his hands through his hair, his eyes deeply troubled. "I can't begin to apologise for what's happened tonight. I feel truly terrible. And embarrassed."

"It's okay, Mason. It's not your fault." I peered over his shoulder. "I don't get what he meant by saying I smell of fae." My face heated once again. Whatever it was, it was cruel and condemning from the way he said it.

Mason sighed. "Back in his day, he was involved in a brief, but bloody battle between shifters and fae. Though they've settled their differences, some of the older ones on both sides maintain prejudices."

I dropped my head. "I see. I take it he was on the shifter side?"

"Yes. We don't tend to trust the fae too much."

"Okay, but I still don't understand why he's connected me to them." I turned to the door. "Look, I'd better go."

I turned the latch and stepped out into the cool night air.

"Are you sure I can't give you a ride back home?"

I shook my head. "Thanks, but I'm fine. You'd better re-join your family."

Mason locked eyes with me. I could feel a wash of emotions that came from him and I inhaled sharply. Then he leaned forward. Any second now and his face would be by my lips. A part of me desperately wanted him to kiss me, but the sensible side that wanted to protect my heart leapt into defence and I jerked my head backwards.

"Mason…." I breathed, my voice husky.

He peeled something off my collar. "You had a little leaf stuck there."

"Oh." I lowered my eyes, feeling like a fool to think he was going to kiss me.

The sound of a car approached, and I squinted as the headlights washed over me.

"Your carriage awaits." He said, softly.

"But I hadn't called anyone."

He gave me a crooked smile. "What good is it having a friend for a wizard if I can't use a little magic now and then?"

I chewed my lip. "Thank you." I stepped forward. "Goodnight, Mason. I'm sorry for the trouble I caused."

He shook his head and winked. "Girl, I knew you were trouble from the first moment I laid eyes on you."

I smirked and walked to the taxi.

When I got back home a little while later, I was still troubled by Quentin's reaction to me. While I wanted answers, my feelings for Mason were all over the place. As much as I tried to ignore it, there was no denying that something was happening between us. I decided that it would be best if we stopped seeing each other as friends. Perhaps some space apart would do us both good. I took a breath and let that settle, but every emotion rebelled. The thought of not speaking to him pulled at my heart and I wasn't sure I could bear losing someone who'd become so special to me in the short time we'd known each other.

I tossed and turned that night, weighing up my decision. I didn't want to jump into another relationship, and it would be unfair to give him hope. Perhaps we'd need to have another talk about our friendship. Anyway, my dad was arriving tomorrow, and I'd be plenty occupied then, and wouldn't have to continually weigh up my feelings when it came to Mason Reed.

Atticus groaned loudly and jumped off the bed.

"Where are you going?" I called out.

"How do you expect me to get my sleep in when you're fidgeting like that?" He huffed. "Besides that's also a symptom of fear and emptiness. Maybe it's time take a hard look at what you're debating." He shook his tail and head held high, he trotted off out of the room.

*Great. Just great. I was being lectured by a cat.*

CHAPTER TEN

As much as I loved being in my shop and showing off my jewellery to new customers, I couldn't wait for the day to end. As I expected, Mason had texted me a couple of times to check if I was okay, to which I reassured him that I was fine. Around four o'clock, I called my dad and he told me he was just leaving and would be with me in a couple of hours. I wished him a safe journey.

"Atticus, I've made a dinner reservation to take dad to *Buono* tonight. Is that okay with you?"

"Yah, no problem, as long as there's fresh chicken for me. I'm going over to spend some time with Elara."

Elara was Fleur and Francois's poodle. They'd become good friends and Atticus often kept her company while the Rosgrove's were in their shop.

"Lovely. Make sure you give my love to all of them."

I glanced out of the shop. It was a lot busier today than normal. I'd discovered from posters around the village square that today was special in the Pagan calendar. As the daylight began to fade, lots of women dressed up as witches, walked around the square holding lit candles and posing on the copper plaque underneath which ran the powerful, magic Ley-line. The candlelight gave the square a lovely ambiance.

Atticus was sitting by the back of the shop, so I turned to him. "Have you noticed how many tours there have been today?"

"Yes," he said in a bored tone. "All due to Imbolc."

"Can you explain it again to me?"

"Yes, it's a pagan holiday marking the halfway point between Winter and Spring. Legend has it that if the day is bright and sunny the winter will last longer. A long time ago, rituals were performed on this day for the success of the new farming season, for divine energy to ensure a steady supply of food."

"That's amazing. And why the candles?"

"Really? I thought you read up on it?"

"Briefly, but I prefer your explanation. Continue, please."

"Very well." He stood and stretched and came over to the main window to look out. "The candles represent fire, which is symbolic for the sun. The lighting of fire celebrates the increasing power of the sun over the next six months."

"To ensure a good harvest," I finished, remembering it now.

"Correct."

"You know, I've never known about this festival."

Atticus moved away from the window and passed by me to the back. "Felicity, there are a lot of things you have yet to learn. Don't be too hard on yourself."

I smiled. "That was nice. You weren't sarcastic for once."

He ignored me. "I see someone new is moving into the filthy vamp's old place."

*Creature Comforts*, the veterinary practice, which was owned by Benedict Vincent, the vampire who had been exiled from Agnes, was indeed being taken over by a new owner.

"Yes, I wonder who's bought it. I heard it's opening on Monday though."

A little bit of sadness washed over me when I thought about Benedict. What a fool I was to have fallen for his charms. I shouldn't have been so trusting from the outset.

Atticus disappeared off and I sighed, pushing those painful thoughts away. I walked over to the door and pulled it open, crossing my arms for warmth and taking in the scene. Soon the bare trees that were dotted around the square would be bursting with new leaves and blossom. I couldn't wait to experience Agnes in Springtime, which was my favourite time of year. For me, it was all about new birth and new beginnings, which was apt for this period of my life.

It was then I noticed three women who were heading my way, dressed up in witch costumes and laughing among themselves. They looked to be in their forties. The one in the middle looked my way, caught my eye and raised her candle in a salute.

I grinned and waved back. They made their way over to me.

"Hello," I greeted. "Looks like you ladies are having a lot of fun."

"Oh, we are." She looked around. "Isn't this village just the cutest? An absolute beauty outside London."

"You're from London?" I asked.

"Yes, born and bred." She looked to her two friends who smiled and nodded along.

"Angie is also celebrating her divorce coming through." Said the one on the left, with the mid-length brown hair.

"Oh, ok…well, congratulations?"

Angie laughed. "Thank you, it certainly is a good day. I'm finally free of Jimmy." She cheered and raised her candle to the sky laughing and her friends did the same.

Their joy was contagious, and I laughed alongside

them. "So, I take it you're here for Imbolc? Are you staying a while?"

Angie replied. "Yes, I've always wanted to come for this festival, but Jimmy thought it was too woo-woo. I wish we could stay longer but we're only here until Sunday." She jerked her head over her shoulder. "We're staying at the *Pern* B&B just outside this lovely square. But next time I know to book in for longer." She smiled. "I run my own boutique in London, and let's just say that my assistant, who's looking after the shop, isn't the most reliable."

"Molly will open the shop, though, won't she?" The other friend enquired, who had her blonde hair tied back in a low ponytail.

"She'd better, Clare. I'm paying her well enough."

Angie turned to me. "Okay, well, we're going to join the last tour of the day. It was nice to say hello." She peered over my shoulder. "We'll be back tomorrow to see some of that lovely jewellery in your shop. By the way, I'm Angela, this is Rose and Clare." She pointed to each of her friends in turn.

"Nice to meet you. I'm Felicity. And I look forward to seeing you all tomorrow. Have fun!" I waved them off and stepped back into my shop, shutting out the cold air.

. . .

After I closed up for the day, I rushed upstairs and took a quick shower. Then I dried my hair and looked out the window into the square. It was bustling and filled with candlelight from the visitors to Agnes. It looked truly magical. As I looked into the crowd, I could have sworn that I saw Becky Scarborough, the owner of The River Inn. But she disappeared into the crowd before I could get a better look at her. But if it was Becky, then it was great that she was back from London. Now that we had banished the malevolent spirit, she would be able to redecorate her B&B and get on with her life.

Just after six o'clock the buzzer to my flat went and my dad, George, announced himself.

"Atticus, he's here!"

I flew down the stairs and threw open the door. My dad stood there with an overnight bag by his feet and his arms already outstretched. He had a great tan from his time in Spain, and judging by his flatter stomach, he'd obviously eaten healthily while abroad. My eyes filled with tears.

"Dad," My voice broke and I threw myself at him.

He laughed out loud and grabbed me into a hug.

"I've missed you so much," I said, the tears now flowing freely from my eyes.

"You too, kiddo. It's so good to see you." He stroked the back of my head like he did when I was a child, which only resulted in more sobbing on my part. Now that he was actually here, I couldn't believe we'd been apart for so long. Or how much had happened to me over the past few months. It was almost as though I'd unconsciously bottled everything up until now and a dam of emotions had broken within me.

"It's okay, darling," he said in a soothing, but slightly worried voice. "I'm here now. And I'm ready to whisk you back to Guildford if this place is upsetting you that much."

I managed to laugh and eventually pulled away from him. "It's not that, I love it here. But it's also not the same without you." I smiled and wiped the last of my tears from my eyes. "Come on, let me show you around. I'll give you the tour of the shop later as it's a separate entrance."

"Oh, I had a peek in the window already. I'm so proud of you, love. It looks amazing."

"Thanks, Dad." He followed me into the small hallway and up the stairs into my flat.

"Well, this is it." I held out my hands and tried to view it from his eyes. A small but inviting living room, led to the open plan kitchen at the other end. The corridor to the left of the stairs led to the bathroom and two bedrooms, one of which I had set up as my office. But I'd made up the spare bed in preparation for his arrival. "Let me give you the quick tour. Oh, and of course, you must meet Atticus, my cat."

"This looks lovely, Flick. It's newly decorated, right?" He walked around the living room, admiring the place. I'd made sure to tuck away my cauldron and bottles of magical herbs and oils deep into a spare cupboard.

I folded my arms and looked around with pride. "Yep."

He smiled and nodded his head. "I much prefer this to your last flat in Clapham. That was such a shoebox in comparison."

I laughed and motioned for him to follow me down to the bedrooms. "That's London for you, Dad."

"Just give me a minute, love." He brought his hands up to his face and sneezed loudly.

"Are you okay?"

"Yes, fine. Come on, where's my room, then?"

I showed him my bedroom first. Atticus was lying on the bed but poked his head up. "Dad, this is my cat, Atticus."

"What a strong name. Lovely looking cat."

I could see the pride in Atticus's eyes. Then Dad covered his face and sneezed again, this time three or four times.

"Dad?"

The next moment he started to rub his eyes which were quickly turning red.

"Flick, I hate to say this and it's very strange, but I think I may be allergic to your cat."

I turned to Atticus, who now looked alarmed and then back to my dad. Disappointment flooded through me. I was so excited to have him stay with me.

But then he broke out into another fit of sneezing and we dashed back into the front room, where I threw open the window. Then I quickly got him glass of water and an antihistamine table.

"Flick, I'm so sorry, darling, but I don't think I can stay here with you."

CHAPTER ELEVEN

"Mr Knight, it's a pleasure to meet you."

Lottie reached across the desk and shook his hand.

"You're in room four. It's the only one I had available.

"It's also happens to be the room I stayed in when I first arrived in Agnes."

Lottie winked at me. "It must be fate." She handed over the key to my dad. "Let me know if you need anything.

We thanked her and then headed up the stairs. Thankfully, Lottie had the room available at the *Serene Stay*. Pern B&B, just off the square which was owned by Victoria Pern was full. Due to Imbolc, she'd put on a special offer and therefore all the rooms were snapped up.

"I'm so sorry, Dad." I watched from the doorway as he placed his bag on the bed. The room brought back fond memories, and everything was in the same place as when I last stayed here. "I had no idea you had a cat allergy."

"Nor did I." He grinned. "But we're all sorted now, so not to worry." The tablet had worked fast, and his eyes were no longer red. Plus the sneezing had stopped as soon as we left my flat. Dad placed his hands on his waist and looked around. Then he went and tried the sink in the en suite. He always did that wherever we stayed.

"Running water okay in these parts?" I asked with an amused tone to my voice. "Not too hard, or soft for you?"

He chuckled and turned off the tap. "Always best to check these things before you settle in for the night."

I stepped into the room and saw him get a little comb out of his trouser pocket. His dark brown hair was finer at the top of his head, but he still had a good amount on the sides. He carefully combed his hair.

"Looking good, dad."

"Thanks, kiddo." He slipped the comb back into his pocket. "Right, fancy some dinner?"

"I've already thought of that." I pulled up my sleeve to check my watch. "You're in for a treat. Come on, I'm taking you to dinner."

∼

*Buono* was packed by the time we entered. A combination of it being one of the best restaurants in the area, and also unusually busy for the horde of tourists which had arrived today. I was glad I decided to make a reservation earlier.

We stood at the entrance of the restaurant and waited for Maria to greet us.

After a few minutes, she came over with a warm and welcoming smile.

"Good evening, Felicity." She looked up at my Dad. "Is this your father?"

"He is, indeed." I glanced at him. "This is George. Dad, please meet Maria."

My Dad extended a hand to her. "It's a pleasure to meet you. I've heard so much about you."

Was it me, or did a pink flush spread across Maria's face?

"I hope it's good, in that case." She smiled coyly at my Dad.

"Nothing but," he hit back, giving her a wink.

Oh, my goodness. I stifled a giggle. I'd rarely seen my dad openly flirt with another woman before. Not in my presence anyway.

Maria picked up a couple of menus and walked us over to a table by the window.

We settled ourselves into our seats and then she told us

about her specials for the evening which, among other dishes, included Calzone.

"The Calzone it is," my dad replied, without even checking the menu.

I raised a brow. "Don't you want to see what else there is?"

He shook his head, but his eyes were on Maria. "No, Maria looks like a woman of fine taste. I'll go with her recommendation. And Maria, feel free to surprise us with your starters too."

She beamed back at him. "Thank you, George." Finally, she dragged her eyes away from him. "Felicity?"

I shut my menu. "Calzone sounds amazing. I'll have the same, please."

"Perfecto. Shall I bring over a wine menu?"

"Just a glass of your best house red, please." Dad replied. "Is that okay for you, Felicity?"

I nodded. I didn't fancy drinking too much.

"I'll be back shortly." Maria took the menus and swept away with a wide smile on her face.

I grinned at Dad.

"What?" He said.

I shrugged. "Nothing."

As I predicted, dinner was incredible, and he was most impressed. After we finished our pudding, which we had to force down considering the very generous potions

Maria served, Dad sat back in his chair and patted his stomach. "That was an absolute feast fit for a King."

"I don't think I can move," I said, groaning.

Maria came over and grinned at our empty plates. "Did you enjoy your apple pie?" Dad nodded. "That was incredible, Maria. I don't think I've eaten a better Italian meal in my life. Thank you."

Maria picked up our plates and expertly stacked them. "You're welcome here anytime, George. As is your lovely daughter, but she knows that anyway. How long are you planning on staying in Agnes?

George glanced at me. "Well, I'll be here for the next few days at least."

I joined my hands together in prayer form. "Unless of course, I can convince Dad to stay."

Maria looked at him. "Is that an option?"

Dad glanced at me and smiled. "I'm not sure I could uproot my entire life back in Guildford where I live, but I'm happy to visit as often as I can."

"That's a shame," Maria said, with a little smile. Then she got all flustered and told us she'd bring us the bill.

"She's pretty, isn't she?" I said to Dad as we watched her rush away.

Dad chuckled. "Now, now, Missy. Don't be getting any ideas." He wagged a finger at me. After we paid up - Dad insisted - even though I wanted to treat him, we thanked

Maria again (Dad left her a very generous tip) and then slipped on our coats as we made our way back outside.

I shivered and zipped up my jacket. "It's such a shame you're allergic to Atticus. I hate that you have to stay in a B&B."

"I'll be fine, love. It looks lovely and Lottie seems rather nice?"

I linked my arm into his. "Oh, it is, and yes, she's lovely but I wish you could stay with me."

We walked down the little side lane, which would take us to the main square.

"Fancy a little walk or are you tired?"

"Definitely a walk, I need to burn off some of this delicious food."

We walked around the square and I pointed out the shops and told him about the owners.

"You love it here, don't you?" He asked with an amused tone to his voice. "I don't think I've ever seen you this happy."

Dad stopped and held me at arm's length.

"What?" I asked.

He narrowed his eyes. "There's something different about you, Flick. I can't place my finger on it, but..." He smiled. "It's like you have this aura about you."

I shrugged it off and smiled. "It's just 'cos you haven't seen me in a long time."

He released me and pressed his lips to my forehead. "No, it's not that. But whatever it is, I'm happy for you."

We continued our walk down the little lanes around the square for a little bit before he spoke again. "I'm not sure how I feel about all this supernatural stuff, though. Don't you think it's a bit odd?"

I tensed slightly. All evening I'd been wrestling with the decision to tell him about my ancestry. "I quite like it?"

"Hmmm..." He furrowed his brows at the couple of people who walked past us laughing dressed in their witch outfits. "I'm glad you're not into all that, Flick."

I bit my lip. My revelation would have to wait for now as I'm not sure he would be able to handle it.

Finally, we'd come around to the back of my shop, where the little streets were less well-lit than the main square in front.

"What's that?" I pointed up ahead to where a sizeable lump, covered in shadow, was on the ground.

I sped up and walked ahead of my dad but as I neared, my heart began to thump.

Dad called out to me. "Flick? Hold on, would you?"

But I couldn't and I rushed forward. The lump on the ground was in fact a body.

I recognised that face.

I threw my hands over my mouth. It was the lady I'd met earlier outside my shop, who was celebrating her divorce. Angie. She was still in her witch costume from earlier, with her discarded candle lying next to her splayed hand. I slowly bent down.

"Angie? Are you okay?"

But I knew it was futile. Her eyes were wide open and glassy.

"Angie?" I called her name again. "Please, say something. Can you hear me?"

She was very much dead.

CHAPTER TWELVE

"Oh my God, is she…"

I held onto my dad's arm and stepped back. "Yes," I whispered. "She's dead."

"Oh, Christ. Poor woman."

"Dad, I need to call the police."

"Yeah, of course. Try not to touch her, love. It's a crime scene now."

"I know, Dad."

We looked around but there wasn't anyone in the street. I pulled out my phone from my pocket and called Desmond's personal mobile.

"Felicity? To what do I owe your call at this time of night?"

"Desmond." I said, hurriedly. "You need to come over

to the square. I've just found a dead body near the back of my shop."

"Don't touch anything." His tone was immediately brusque and formal. "I'll be there as fast as I can." He hung up before I had a chance to say anything else.

"Do you want to sit in my shop, while I wait for Officer Desmond to arrive?"

"And leave you out here alone when there's a murderer about? You've got to be joking."

I wondered where Angie's friends were. If I recalled correctly, their names were Clare and Rose. Were they back at the B&B? And if so, why was Angie out here on her own? To be fair, there were still people out and about in the main square with their candles. But a lot of them would be celebrating in the warmth of the Mystical Moon, next to the roaring open fireplace. It was just out here, along these back lanes, that were mostly deserted at this time of night.

As the street was narrow, Desmond wasn't able to drive his car down to us, so he parked at the top, close to the location of Angie's body. He left his bright lights on, which shone down the path.

"He's here," I said to Dad. "Come on."

We rushed forward to meet Desmond.

"Desmond, this is my father, George."

Both men briefly nodded at each other. I continued.

"We were out for dinner at *Buono* and decided to go for a walk and work it off. A few minutes ago, we stumbled upon the body."

"Please lead the way," Desmond said, turning on his torch to add more light.

"This way." I turned and walked the hundred or so yards back to Angie's body, with Desmond on my heels and my Dad behind him.

Then I stopped and pointed at Angie's body. Desmond shone his torch on her.

I gasped. Her neck was red and bruised. Thrown next to her body was what looked like a piece of black cord.

"Looks like the cause of death is strangulation but of course I'll need to get an autopsy." He turned to look at me. "Do you know the victim by any chance?"

"I don't but I saw her in the square earlier today, with two of her friends. They stopped outside my shop for a little chat. Her name is Angie."

Desmond pulled out his notepad and scribbled across it. "Thanks."

"She mentioned she was staying at the *Pern* B&B. I wonder if her friends are back there?"

"I need to make a couple of calls, but I can take it from here." He looked at me and nodded. "Thanks for your help."

I released a staggering breath. "Poor woman. She said she was celebrating her divorce."

We all turned to look at her. What a nightmare end for her.

My Dad insisted that I go inside my flat and lock the door, while he waited outside and watched. He wouldn't know, but I muttered a few words and threw up a quick protection ward around him.

"Are you sure I can't walk you back to the *Serene Stay*?"

"No. You stay here and be safe. I'll be fine, it's only a ten-minute walk, if that."

I gave him a fierce hug. "Okay, text me when reach, Dad. Love you."

"Will do. Love you too, Flick. I'll see you in the morning." We pulled apart and he motioned for me to go inside.

He was a lot more sombre than earlier, but it was to be expected. I hated that he'd always have this memory of his first night in Agnes. I watched him walk away from the spy hole in my door, until he was out of sight, and then I raced upstairs.

"Atticus! Are you here?" I called out.

"In here, where's the fire? Do I need to leave now?"

I ran into the bedroom, where I saw him lying across my bed. I flipped on the light.

"Could you give me some warning?" He squinted. "Have a little respect for the baby-blues."

"I just found a dead body," I blurted out.

"Whoa. Okay, I'm officially awake."

I stepped into the room and flopped down onto the bed.

Atticus stood up and stretched. "Tell me."

"It was a lady I met earlier outside the shop." I told him about meeting Angie, Clare and Rose. And then the finding of her body.

"She seemed so happy, earlier," I said furrowing my brows. "Who would do this to her?"

"Terribly unfortunate. How did George take it?"

"I think he's in a bit of a shock. I did a quick protection and calming spell on him when he just left. I think he'll sleep well at least."

"I'm sorry he couldn't stay. I was going to offer to move out for a few days."

"Atticus." I stroked his head. "You'd do that?"

"Well, I was hoping it wouldn't come to that."

I shook my head and narrowed my eyes at him. "So you were, or you weren't?"

He sighed. "Fine. I asked Wilma if I could sleep in her witch's shed if it was absolutely necessary."

"That's kind of you." I pressed my lips together and joined my hands on my lap. "I've never known my Dad to be allergic to any animal in my life."

"What are you trying to imply?"

I turned to Atticus. "Nothing, I just think it's odd."

"It's the magic." He replied, settling down on the bed once more. "It's too strong in here."

I widened my eyes. "You think so?"

"I'd hedge my bets. Sometimes a John Doe can't be among a witch and a familiar."

"I see."

"It's for the best, anyway."

"Why"

"Well, you're going to do some investigating of your own, aren't you? We may need to do some spell work."

A smile tugged at the corners of my mouth. "I wasn't sure I was planning on getting involved."

"Oh, please, Felicity. You know full well that, since you discovered that poor woman's body, you're not going to just ignore it."

"I guess you know me better than I know myself." Atticus was right. Someone took away that poor woman's life and short-lived happiness. They deserved to pay for their heinous crime. "Do you feel like coming along for a walk?"

"Now?"

"Yes, I'm going to see if I can find Clare and Rose."

"Fine."

"Fine. Hurry!"

Atticus was up in record time and we left our flat and headed in the direction of the *Pern* B&B, which was just outside the square and in the opposite direction to *The River Inn* B&B. It was past ten now and as we approached, I saw a parked police car outside. We quickly took cover in the shadows and peeked out from where we were.

Atticus groaned after a few minutes. "Oh, for goodness' sake, what do you think you're going to achieve by us standing by this building?"

"I was waiting to see if anyone was coming out of the B&B, actually" I snapped.

"Well, I do have better things to do with my evening."

"Such as?"

Atticus huffed and began to walk forward.

"Wait. Where are you going?"

He stopped and turned to me. "I'm going to walk over and see if I can hear anything. Is that okay with you?"

"Yes, fine but also, I don't know why you're being so grumpy tonight."

He ignored me and sauntered off. I watched the *Pern* B&B for any signs of movement but there was nothing. However, as Atticus approached the building, he dropped into the shadows as the door pushed open and a policeman and two women stepped out.

I tried to crane my neck to see if I could recognise the

policeman, but he was an elderly man, and I definitely hadn't seen him before in Agnes. Next to him the two women were standing with their heads bent down. They were no longer dressed in their witch costumes, but I could tell it was Clare and Rose, Angie's friends. All three of them were too preoccupied in their discussion to notice Atticus who cleverly hung by the building, pretending to groom his paw.

From where I was standing, I couldn't hear a thing they were saying but the conversation continued for the next few minutes, and then the older policeman passed them something, which looked like his card. He placed a hand on both their shoulders in turn and then got into his car and turned on the engine. As he slowly drove off, the two women clung to each other, their shoulders shaking.

CHAPTER THIRTEEN

After a few minutes, as I watched, the two women pulled apart and said something to each other. I wanted to go over and offer them my condolences and help, but at the same time I was wary of interfering with the police investigation. Also, Atticus was still there and I'm sure he would pass on whatever he heard. It was another few minutes when, shaking their heads, the women quickly glanced around and then went back into the building. Once they disappeared, Atticus made his way back to me.

I rushed forward. "Atticus, did you catch everything they said?"

"I did. Shall I tell you, or would you like to see my memories?"

"Your memories, if you're okay with that."

We hurried away from the *Pern* B&B and walked in the direction of the river. Once we were there, we walked a little until we found a secluded spot, that wouldn't be visible to anyone walking along at this time of night. Atticus stood at the water's edge, with me next to him, and then he touched the side of his head and dipped the same paw into the water.

Atticus had only done this once before, and I found it fascinating to see how he was able to pull his memories from his brain to provide a picture for me. As I watched it, the water began to swirl, and a mist began to form. The ripples turned green, and daylight poured into the spot. A scene began to appear. It was through Atticus's eyes, and he glanced at both the policeman and at Angie's friends.

"Once again, ladies, I'm so sorry to inform you of your friend's death. It's exceedingly rare to have such a crime like this in Agnes. If there is anything you can think of, as we discussed, please don't hesitate to get in touch." The two women nodded.

"I don't officially work at the police station anymore, as technically I'm retired, but I always like to help with big cases such as this, so you're welcome to call me any time. The main officer in charge of this case will be Detective Desmond Grey." He reached into his pocket and pulled out business cards, which he passed to Clare and Rose.

"We'll find out who did this to your friend. I promise."

Then women nodded holding onto each other. Rose brushed some tears away from her eyes. "Thank you."

Then he got into his car and drove off. The two women looked at each other.

"Why didn't you tell him about Jimmy?" Clare said to Rose.

"We can't just go around accusing people, you know."

Clare sighed and rubbed her arms. I'm sorry, you're right. Let's sleep on it and see what we think in the morning. Anyway, we have to meet Officer Grey tomorrow for our official statements. I'm glad Officer Townsend was okay with a verbal one for tonight." Her voice cracked. "I can't believe Angie's gone."

They started to cry and gripped each other for a few minutes.

"Come on," Rose finally said, pulling apart. "Let's go inside. It might not be safe out here."

The scene began to fade away, the colour evaporated, and the water was back to a dark, gurgling river.

I released a slow and staggered breath. "I think that was Thomas Townsend. Desmond's former boss. He told me the other day that Officer Townsend still likes to keep tabs on what's happening in Agnes." I glanced around to see if anyone could have spotted us, but it was still quiet at this end of the river. "Thank you, Atticus."

"You're welcome. I was beginning to think I was losing my uses for you."

"What do you mean?"

"Well, you're so taken with all your new friends of late, and Mason of course." He looked down at the ground and I bent down and scooped him up into my arms. That would likely explain why he'd been so grumpy with me of late. "And now George is here…I'm beginning to think my days are numbered."

*Always so dramatic.* I bit back a smile. "Come on now, Atticus. You know you're still my number one," I said in a soothing voice as I began to walk.

He raised his big blue eyes up at me. "Forever?"

"Well, if you keep behaving."

∼

The following morning, I looked up as the bell to the shop door jangled.

"Dad! What are you doing here so early?" I walked around my counter to greet him. He was holding two Starbucks take-away cups.

I took the one he handed me and placed it on the counter, giving him a kiss on the cheek. "Thank you, this is great."

"I've been up ages, love. Been out for my morning run.

Vanilla latte, is that still what you like, or have you changed your poison since moving here?"

"No, this is perfect." I took a sip of the delicious brew and smacked my lips together in appreciation. "How did you sleep?"

Dad walked forward to my display counter and sat his coffee down. "Very well, thank you. The bed was heavenly. And Lottie serves a delicious breakfast."

"Good, and yes, I remember. So, you run nowadays?"

Dad laughed and patted his stomach. "Well, I had to figure out a way to get rid of this paunch. I've been running for a few months now. Simon got me into it."

Simon was one of the group of friends that he had been travelling with in Spain over the last few months. "I like him then, he's a good influence."

Dad looked around the shop. "Flick, I love what you've done in here. So, are you going to give me a tour?"

I smiled. "Of course." I spread my arms out and did a little spin on the spot. "So, this is me."

I pointed into the cabinet which was in front of us. Dad bent down and peered into the glass walls.

"This is where I display all my latest collections." I pointed to the right of him. "Over there, I generally tend to put special offers on those display stands or if I have anything on sale."

Dad stood up and walked around the shop. "I like your

taste, Flick. I knew you were destined for greater things than just working as a secretary in an office."

"Thank you, Dad," I said softly. "If it wasn't for the money, you'd put aside for me, I could have never had this."

He waved off my comment and had a good look at all my jewellery collections. "I know I'm biased when I say this, but you really are talented. You deserve to show it off."

On one end of the room, I had a vintage style bookshelf, where I sold books on various types of healing crystals and other metaphysical subjects.

He looked over the titles. "You've always been into your rather unusual interests, haven't you?" His tone was mildly amused as he took a sip of his coffee.

I laughed but it sounded a little nervous even to my ears. "Yeah, well…"

We caught up a little about the business, and I shared my accounting books with him. Dad seemed to be impressed and pleased with my profits. Then, as I knew it would, the conversation turned to the discovery of Angela's body from last night.

"I still can't believe what happened to that poor woman last night." He said, shaking his head sombrely.

"I know, I only met her yesterday."

Dad raised a brow. "You knew her?"

"Oh no," I shook my head. "I was standing outside the shop, yesterday afternoon, when she walked past with her two friends. We got chatting. I knew her for all of five minutes."

"I still can't get the image of her body out of my head. I thought I'd be tossing and turning all night, but somehow I slept like a log." He scratched the top of his head. "How are you holding up?"

I shrugged. "Same as you. Feel terrible about what happened to her. Did Lottie say anything to you this morning?"

"No, I don't think she knows yet, but I suspect that, since this a small village, news will travel fast."

Yes," I said sadly. "I hope they'll catch her killer soon."

"Do they have a good police department here?" He enquired.

*Yes, because I help to solve the crimes.* "Yes, definitely. Officer Desmond Grey is good at what he does. Plus, I hear that his former boss who's semi-retired, helps out now and then. I'm sure they'll be all over the case."

"Good. I hate the thought of you living in a village without adequate police protection."

The door jangled once again and we both turned to look to see who had come in.

Both Clare and Rose stood hesitantly at the door. Their eyes were swollen and bloodshot.

CHAPTER FOURTEEN

"It's Felicity, isn't it?" Rose, the one with the mid-length brown hair who I met yesterday, stepped forward.

"Yes," I replied. I shot a quick glance at my Dad and stepped around my counter to greet them.

The two women looked at each other hesitantly. Rose spoke again. "We heard that you found Angie's body last night."

Her eyes filled with tears and her friend, Clare, gripped onto Rose's arm. Neither of them looked like they'd slept at all. Clare's long blonde hair was a tangled mess.

I nodded. "I'm so, very sorry." I said, quietly.

"Can we ask," Claire said, her voice breaking. "Where was Angie when you found her?"

I saw my Dad looking at the two women with deep concern in his face. "This is my father, George, who's visiting me. We had dinner last night and then walked around for a bit catching up. That's when we stumbled upon Angie's body." I lowered my head. "She was in the street at the back of my shop."

"I'm so sorry for your loss," my dad said softly.

Tears fell from Clare's eyes, and I quickly walked behind my display unit and grabbed a box of tissues. I handed the box to her and she accepted a tissue gratefully, dabbing at her eyes. Rose appeared to be holding it together for now.

"I can't believe I only met her yesterday. She was so full of life, and happy to be here."

"She is, I mean, was." Rose replied. "Angie had been looking forward to coming to Agnes for quite some time now. We planned this weekend for ages."

"Do you have any suspicions about who could have attacked her?"

Clare's eyes widened. "No, why would you say that?"

I shook my head. "Oh no, I didn't mean anything by that." I wanted to ask them about someone called Jimmy, who I'd overheard them discussing via Atticus last night, but obviously I couldn't say anything.

"It's okay," Clare said. "I don't know anybody who'd

would want to hurt Angie. She was such a lovely and caring woman."

"Anyone from her past?" I prodded.

Rose glared at me. "I'm not sure what you're trying to get at, Felicity."

I bit my lip. "I'm sorry, I didn't mean to offend you. I guess I'm just trying to help you figure out who would want to do this to Angie. Although of course, you two knew her better than anyone else. I didn't mean to be nosey."

Rose shared a look with Clare. Clare gave her a little nod and then they both turned back to me. "Angie's ex-husband, Jimmy, was quite a jealous man." Rose said.

"I see." I raised a brow. "Do you think he could have been a threat to her?"

Claire shrugged her shoulders. "We're not too sure. But I know that they had a big row recently, over some assets, but I suppose it's to be expected with an acrimonious divorce, which theirs was."

Rose glanced at around my shop. "Angie was one of our best friends, but she was also very private about her personal life. We had no idea that she and Jimmy were having such bad marital problems, until one day she broke down and told us that she couldn't take it anymore. That's when she filed for separation, but we know that Jimmy didn't take it too well."

"Did Jimmy know that you were here for the weekend in Agnes?"

"Angie didn't say," Clare replied. She glanced at her watch. "Anyway, we're just on our way to the police station, but we were a little lost, so we thought we'd stop in here since we met you yesterday and ask you for directions."

"Of course," I said. I walked over to the door and pulled it open. The three of us stepped out into the cool morning air. I pointed them in the direction of the local police station, where I knew Desmond would be waiting to take their statement.

I folded my arms across my chest to keep warm. "This has been a huge shock to all of us, and again I'm so sorry for what's happened to your dear friend, Angie. If there is anything I can do to help, please don't hesitate to ask."

Their eyes once again filled with tears and Rose roughly brushed hers away. "This was supposed to be our amazing girls' weekend away." She snorted. "Now I wish we'd never come to Agnes. Angie would still be alive."

I pressed my lips together and furrowed my brows. What could I say to that? She was right. After all, if Angie hadn't come here, she would most likely still be alive.

"Again, I'm so sorry for your loss."

The two ladies nodded. "Thank you," Clare replied. "We'll be on our way now, and if officer Grey doesn't need us to stay, we're going to see if we can try and get back to London this afternoon."

I watched them walk off in the direction of the police station, and then I entered back into my shop, firmly closing the door behind me. I shivered.

"Are you okay, love?" My dad enquired.

"I feel so sorry for them." I walked over to my display unit and took a couple of sips of my coffee which was now stone cold. I'd been so engrossed in showing Dad around my shop and talking about my business that I had completely forgotten about it.

"What are your plans for today?" I asked him.

"I think I'll have a little wander around."

"You must pop into Rosgrove Cheese and Wine shop."

"Anything special about them?"

I nodded enthusiastically. "I know you like your red wine, so trust me when I say you won't find anything better in England."

Dad gave me an amused smile. "Well in that case, I shall definitely have a look." He stood up from his stool and stretched.

"The owners, Fleur and Francois, are actually good friends of mine. They're really nice people. Tell them I sent you."

"Will do, Flick." He shrugged his jacket back on. "I'll let

you get on for now, but I'll pop back in a bit, and perhaps we can go and get some lunch together?"

"Definitely, have a good wander around, Dad."

I felt bad that I had to work while he was over for the weekend, but I knew he wouldn't want me to shut the shop on his account. He gave me a little wave and stepped out into the cool air.

The rest of the morning was fairly quiet. I caught up with my admin, and a couple of orders which I had to process. It also gave me time to put together a few bracelets and a couple of simple necklaces. I hadn't seen Atticus for most part of the morning, so I assumed he was still upstairs snoozing. I didn't blame him; it wasn't the best weather to be out and about.

A little while later, the door opened and I looked up from my paperwork, to see my good friend, Lucy, standing there. She rushed over to me.

"Felicity, I heard the news. Are you alright?"

"I'm fine." I gave her a weak smile. "I take it you heard from Desmond?"

Officer Grey was Lucy's older half-brother. "I did," she nodded. "I gave him a call this morning for a catch up, but he seemed unusually busy. I immediately knew something was up."

"Let me guess, you got him to tell you what was going on?"

Lucy had a great way of persuading her brother for titbits of information. "He did, eventually. Besides, he knew I'd hear about it anyway. And," she glanced out of the shop window, "I suspect it won't be long before everyone will be talking about it today.

I sighed. "It's so sad, I can't believe this happened here on such a special day."

Lucy scrunched her brows. "You mean the witch festival thingy?"

I nodded. "There were so many people in the square yesterday, candles everywhere. Who knows what type of people the festival brought to the village?"

Lucy nodded glumly. "I hope Desmond will find the killer soon. Also, he mentioned that Thomas Townsend is assisting him with the case, so hopefully it won't be long before justice is served."

"Let's hope so."

We caught up for a little bit and then I asked her how she was getting on with her boyfriend, Gareth. They had recently moved in together.

Lucy's face took on a dreamy look. "He's the best boyfriend I could ever ask for."

I smiled. I was thrilled for her as Lucy had been through a lot recently. "And how are things with your mother?" I asked tentatively.

The smile on her face vanished. "The same."

I knew it would take some time for their relationship to heal. Before I could say anything, Lucy's face brightened up once again.

"By the way, I met your dad earlier."

"You did? Where?"

"I was picking up a bottle of wine and some of their delicious cheese from Fleur when I overheard George talking to Francois, and he mentioned you. Naturally, I went over and introduced myself as your absolute best friend in the village."

I grinned. "I'm so glad you got a chance to meet him."

"He's absolutely lovely. You're so lucky, Felicity."

"I know," I said with pride. "I'm glad you ran into him, he said he was pottering about for a bit. You would have met him tonight anyway, but now I'm also wondering if I should still go ahead with the meet-up?"

"Of course, you should."

I had arranged for a get-together at the Mystical Moon this evening with some close friends that I wanted Dad to meet. However, with the sad news about Angie's murder, I didn't know if it was appropriate, even though I barely knew the woman.

"You must." Lucy interrupted my thoughts as if reading my mind. "Besides, George is only here for a day or two, it would be a shame for you not to introduce him to your friends."

"You're right." I paused. "By the way, I need to stop into your shop and pick up some cans of food for Atticus. He's eating me out of house and home with his demands for fresh roast chicken." I rolled my eyes. Lucy owned *Happy Paws*, the pet shop in the village, and sold some lovely organic cat food, which Atticus favoured.

Before she could reply, we both turned to the door, as a delivery man stepped into the shop, looking around. He was carrying a gigantic bouquet of flowers in his hands.

CHAPTER FIFTEEN

"Hello," he said smiling. "I'm looking for Felicity Knight."

I shot Lucy a quick, confused look. And stepped forward. "Hi, that's me."

The delivery man stepped into the shop and proceeded to hand me the huge bouquet of flowers. I rested them in my arms as I took in the beautiful long stemmed pink roses, which were mixed with a variety of different seasonal flowers and foliage. It was the most beautiful bouquet I'd ever seen in my life."

He must have noticed my bulging eyes and chuckled. "You're a lucky lady. I've never had the pleasure of delivering such a big bunch before."

"Thank you."

He turned and gave me a little wave. "Enjoy. Just as

well my wife hasn't seen them, wouldn't want to give her any ideas."

As soon as he left the shop, Lucy squealed. "Felicity Knight, what aren't you telling me?" She folded her arms across her chest.

"Um, nothing? I've no idea who these are from."

"Why don't you read the card then?"

I swallowed and pulled out the small white envelope, which was stuck on the outside of the wrapper. Lucy hovered over my shoulder. I quickly scanned the card:

*Felicity, I'm so sorry about the other night. I hope you'll forgive us and come back another time. M*

Lucy let out a low whistle. "And who is *M*?" She asked with a raised eyebrow.

A small smile played across my lips. "He's a friend. Mason Reed."

"And how come you've never mentioned him before?"

Thankfully, Lucy had been preoccupied with moving into her new home with Gareth, a few weeks ago, so she was completely unaware of my incident with Raphael. I told her that I had scratched my neck with some jewellery, which is why I had been wearing the bandage.

"I met him recently, at Lara's New Year's Eve party." I shrugged my shoulder casually. I didn't really know what else to tell her, because the truth was, we were friends and nothing more.

"And will Mason be joining us tonight at the Mystical Moon?"

I had invited Mason a few days ago when I had spoken to my friends about the get-together, but after the events of the other night, I wasn't sure if it would be a good idea. It was obvious his great grandfather, Quentin, didn't approve of me and I had no intention of causing any trouble for him. Then again, it would be cruel to rescind my invitation to him after he's sent me such an incredible bunch of flowers.

"Yes, I think he'll still be coming." I said casually. "I mean, he hasn't said otherwise."

"Cool," Lucy said waggling her eyebrows. "I'm looking forward to meeting this Mason of yours."

I narrowed my eyes at Lucy. "Lucy, don't you start. I told you I am quite happy being single."

"You mean single and ready to *mingle?*" She laughed.

I waved away her comment and tried to give her a stern look, but I couldn't help laughing back with her. Once again, the door opened and there was my dad standing there at the entrance.

"Hello, ladies." He grinned at both of us and then his gaze landed on the flowers. His eyes rounded.

"Whoa."

"Yep," Lucy agreed. "As much as I love Gareth, I can't imagine him buying me a bunch like this." She pouted playfully.

I tucked my hair behind my ears and avoided my dad's gaze. "They're from a friend."

"Riiiight," he replied. From his amused tone, I could tell he wasn't quite sure. Thankfully, he changed the subject.

"Lucy, I've come to whisk my daughter away for lunch. Would you care to join us?"

"Oh no, that's fine, but thank you, George" Lucy spoke to him as if they were old-time friends. "I need to get back to my shop, but I look forward to seeing you soon." She shot me a wink since I'd asked everyone to keep my little get-together a surprise.

"Bye, love." He said, as she walked past and dropped a kiss on his cheek.

"You've got a fan," I said, smiling at Lucy's departing figure.

"What can I say?" He shrugged and curled his lip, faking an Italian accent, Godfather -style. "*Charming* is my middle name."

I rolled my eyes but smiled. "Could you give me a few

minutes, please? I need to run up and put these flowers in water. Plus, I haven't seen Atticus for a while, and I should check he's okay. He'll be screaming blue murder if I don't give him lunch." I'd invite Dad up, but I didn't want to risk causing him another allergic reaction.

"Yeah, if only cats could talk, I'm sure they'd have a few choice words for their humans." he chuckled. "I swear Rory, my neighbour's new cat, always appears to be looking down on me. Unless of course, I give him a scrap of food and then he's pleasant as pie." He brushed away his hair. "Cats, eh?"

I carefully picked up my flowers and headed for the stairs. *If only you knew, Dad.*


I assumed Atticus was sleeping, and I didn't want to call out for him, in case he answered. That would give Dad an awful fright if he heard us conversing. So, I crept up the stairs and headed for the kitchen, where I placed my gorgeous flowers onto the counter. I lowered my head, closed my eyes, and deeply inhaled the scent of the long-stemmed roses. Their perfume was potent and heavenly, like nothing I'd ever smelt before.

The other flowers surrounding the roses were just as beautiful, combinations of pinks and purples. Mason had really outdone himself. A smile played on my lips. I pulled out my phone and sent him a quick message to thank him. We hadn't properly spoken since the other night, and I couldn't help but feel a little nervous excitement at the thought of seeing him later this evening at the pub.

I opened the cupboard quietly and pulled out my biggest vase, which I filled with water, and then I carefully arranged the stems. As I suspected, one vase wasn't enough to hold the amount of flowers Mason had sent, so I had to select a second one for the remaining stems. I stepped back to admire them. They brightened up my flat and looked beautiful. Once I'd placed them where I wanted, I scanned the room to see if I could spot Atticus. I almost jumped out of my skin. Atticus was lying on the rug, peering up at me with one eye slit open. Snoozing next to him was Wilma. My mouth dropped open.

*Quiet.* Atticus commanded as he communicated silently. *Or you'll wake her.*

*What are you doing?*

*Having a rest, what does it look like?*

*Don't be belligerent. What's Wilma doing here?*

Atticus stretched out a paw. *She's having a snooze with me, we're a bit tired after our earlier walk from Lawnes. Do you think next time you'd be able to, maybe, knock?*

I widened my eyes. *Atticus, you are my familiar. Or do I need to remind you? I don't need to knock when I come to see you. Especially since I'm in my own flat.*

He rolled his eyes upwards. *No need to get technical and snippy.*

*So, what's going on?*

*Well, you've just interrupted a very pleasant snooze. In fact, probably the best snooze I've had in years.*

I placed a hand on my hip and cocked my head to the side.

*Are you going now? I'd like to go back to sleep.*

My eyebrows shot up to my hairline. *Really?*

*Yes, do you know how hard it's been to get Wilma over here? Do you realise the extent to which I've had to work my charms for her to fall for me?*

I couldn't help but grin. *You've won her over?*

*I'm getting there. I did as you suggested and told her how I felt. But you're not helping things right now by interrupting our quiet time. I had to mute you with magic to stop you from banging around with those flowers.*

*Do you like them?*

He peered over my shoulder. *Not bad. Let me guess, Mason?*

*How did you know?*

*I'm a lot wiser than you give me credit for. I see what's going on around me.*

*Errr...O-kay then. I guess I'd better get going. Dad's waiting for me downstairs. Oh, Atticus?*

*Yes?*

*Do you want me to put out lunch for you two?*

*I take it that's a rhetorical question. There's enough chicken in the fridge for both of us. Yes, if you could take it out now, it'll be room temperature when we're ready to dine.*

I bit back a retort and took the food out of the fridge as he asked. Then I portioned it into two plates and left it on the ground. On impulse, I grabbed a rose from the vase and placed it next to Wilma's plate. Then I headed back for the door.

I shot him a wink. *Enjoy your snooze. I'll be back later.*

*Don't rush.*

Charming. *Fine.*

*Fine.*

CHAPTER SIXTEEN

*L*ater that evening, I had just finished getting dressed for my night at the Mystical Moon, when the buzzer to the flat went. Atticus raised his head from the sofa.

"I thought you were meeting George at the pub?"

"I am. Everyone's arriving in about ten minutes. I wonder who that could be?"

"Only one way to find out, then." Atticus said. "Be careful, just in case." He followed behind me.

I went down the stairs and peeked out the spy hole.

"Who is it?" Atticus asked.

"Your best human besides me."

I pulled open the door, ignoring the slight flutter in my chest.

"Mason." I smiled as he stood on my doorstep, dressed

in his usual leather jacket. He was wearing black faded jeans and his windswept hair was pushed to the side. He looked like he belonged on the cover of a men's fashion magazine. I sucked in a breath.

"Hi." He ran his gaze up and down my outfit, and I felt the heat rise to my face. "You look great."

I lowered my gaze and smiled. I was wearing my new black jeans, and a lace cream blouse. My hair was twisted up into a chignon, and I wore only a smattering of light make up.

"Thank you," I replied. "Did you get my text earlier?"

"I did, and I'm glad you like the flowers."

"Mason, you're lucky I don't have allergies," Atticus commented, dryly.

I rolled my eyes. "Ignore him, they're absolutely beautiful. Thank you, again."

Mason looked at me intently. "It's nothing."

I cleared my throat. "So, I hadn't heard from you, and I wasn't sure if you were still coming tonight."

"I wouldn't miss it for the world. Plus, I'm really looking forward to meeting George."

I smiled, but my chest was thumping. I was about to introduce him to my father. "Great. Would you give me a sec? I'm just going to go and grab my coat."

"Take your time, I'll just wait here."

. . .

The Mystical Moon was just over a five minutes' walk from my flat.

"Thanks for coming over and walking with me to the pub." I said.

Mason stood close to me as we walked through the square and into the lane. "It's no problem. Also, I don't like the idea of you walking alone on your own, when there's a killer about."

Everyone was talking about Angie's murder. I sighed in response.

"Yeah, it's awful."

"I'm not sure if you saw but it was on the local evening news earlier."

"I did. She seemed so happy when I met her the day before. Life can be so cruel."

"It can. But you can't change the wheels of your destiny, Felicity."

I nodded. We were nearing the pub, and I turned to Mason before we went on further. "Mason, I need to say something."

He stopped and turned to face me. "What's up?"

"You know I really like you as my friend, but I don't want to come between you and your family." I didn't want him to feel obligated to me in any way.

Mason's expression grew serious. "Felicity, I know you just want to be friends; I get it." He flashed me a lopsided smile. "But I really care about you. And as for my great grandfather, he'll come around. Honestly, my mother was so mad at him after you left, and my dad was just as disappointed." He paused and pushed his hair away from his forehead. "They both insisted I tell you that they want to have you over sometime again in the near future, if you're willing to give them another chance. Of course, they'll make sure that great-grandfather Quentin won't be in attendance."

I looked down at my shoes. Why did my heart suddenly feel so heavy? "Thank you, Mason. That means a lot."

We continued the last hundred yards in silence and then Mason reached for the door of the pub and pulled it open. The warmth of the fire enveloped us and as we stepped inside, the door pulled closed behind us.

I waved at Nick, who was behind the bar serving drinks. The pub was already packed, as it normally was on a Saturday evening. Nick waved back and pointed with his finger to his right, where he had reserved a little section for me. I gave him a thumbs up, as Mason and I threaded our way through the tables.

"What would you like to drink?" Mason asked.

"Don't worry, I've arranged with Nick to bring over champagne."

"Very nice, I see you're going all out, Felicity."

"It's not often I get a chance to spoil my friends." I winked at him.

The door opened and my dad walked in, looking around. I waved and he smiled, making his way over to our table.

"Hi, Dad." I moved around the chair and gave him a kiss on the cheek.

"Hello, love. What a lovely place this is."

He hugged me, and then we pulled apart. I glanced at Mason and then took a breath. "Dad, this is my friend, Mason."

Dad held out his hand, and he warmly shook Mason's hand. "Good to meet you, Mason." He clapped his shoulder.

"Likewise, Sir."

My dad burst out laughing. "No need for any formalities, son. You can call me George."

Mason seemed almost shy as he shot me a look and to my dad, he grinned. "George, it is."

Soon our other friends piled into the pub First there was Francois and Fleur, followed by Emma, Darcey and Mia. Soon after, Lucy and Gareth arrived together with Lara and Luca. All my friends were now here and gathered.

Nick had filled up our glasses with champagne, so then I clicked my flute with a spoon to get everyone's attention.

When they all turned to look, I held up my glass, smiling at each one of my friends in turn.

"I'd like to propose a toast. To good friends, good health, and to my wonderful dad, George, who has finally been able to come up and visit me."

"To good friends, health and George!" They all shouted back.

We clicked glasses with each other, and the evening was underway.

I was thrilled to see that Dad had no problem integrating with my friends, and equally, they all seemed to enjoy his stories about his recent travels in Spain. He was enjoying being the centre of attention and was definitely having a good time.

"Your dad is a really brilliant guy." Mason said quietly next to me. He had barely left my side all evening.

I took a sip of my champagne. "Thank you," I looked over at my dad who was deep in conversation with Gareth. "Yep, he is."

"Do you think he'll move here to Agnes?"

"I don't know." I shook my head sadly. "I'd love that more than anything, but I think it's too much for him to uproot his life from Guildford. I tried my best to convince him over lunch yesterday, but I don't think he's as taken with the village as I am."

"Yeah, with Angie's murder, I doubt he's seen it in the best light."

I nodded. It had been on my mind all evening. I'd been thinking if there was any way that I could track Jimmy, Angie's ex-husband. While her murder was none of my business, but since it was me who found her body along with dad, I felt invested. I wondered if her friends were still in Agnes, or if they had left to go back home to London this afternoon as they'd hoped.

"Hey, Felicity?"

I glanced up to see Lucy looking my way.

"What's up?" I asked.

"Did you know that Becky is back?"

My eyes rounded. "I thought I saw her the other day, in the square."

Lucy nodded. "Yep, I bumped into her earlier this evening, but she was in a rush to get on her way. I guess she must have got back from London over the last couple of days. She's probably in shock having seen the state of *The River Inn*."

I agreed with her. A thought occurred to me. I was going to ask Lara discreetly if there was anything we could do to help Becky fix up her place. What with the black mould on the walls and the horrible smell, I hoped Lara would be open to us doing a little sweep of magic over the place to help

Becky restore it back to its original state before the haunting. And, afterwards, perhaps Lara could do a memory spell on Becky so that she wouldn't remember what *The River Inn* was like when she arrived back from London.

Later that evening, after Nick practically begged us to leave so he could close up for the night, we laughed and finally stood up from the table.

"It's been such a fun evening," Mia said coming over to me and hugging me. "Thank you."

"Thank you so much for coming." I kissed her cheek and leaned in closer.

"By the way, you should know that Becky from *The River Inn* is back. I wonder if it's worth for us to go over and do a little sweep, just to make sure that the spirit has definitely gone?"

Mia nodded, and glanced over at Darcey and Emma, who were hugging my Dad goodbye. "Definitely. I'll talk to the girls and text you tomorrow so we can try and figure out a time when to go over."

I'd no idea why, but a sudden chill ran through me.

## CHAPTER SEVENTEEN

*I* insisted on walking dad back to the *Serene Stay*, after we left the pub. He wasn't having any of it, until Mason interjected and suggested he come along with us so that I would also have company on the way back. Dad finally relented. So, we all walked the short distance back to the B&B, my arm linked with his. I loved him being here with me in Agnes. While I'd missed him terribly, having him here made me realise just how much. I hated the thought that he was probably leaving tomorrow, although he hadn't yet confirmed it. He and Mason seemed to really hit it off, though I was kind of dreading dad giving me the third degree about our friendship, as I knew he would.

In no time, we arrived at the *Serene Stay*, and Dad and I made plans to meet in the morning after breakfast.

"Are you planning on leaving tomorrow George?" Mason asked.

Dad glanced at me. "I was considering it, but I'm in two minds. So, I asked Lottie earlier if she still had a room available for a couple more days, which she does." He winked at me. "What do you think, Flick? Should your old man hang around for a bit longer?"

I grinned and threw my arms around his neck. "Thank you, Dad, that would be amazing."

"In that case, Mason, guess I'm here a bit longer."

After we bid our goodnights, Mason and I walked back towards the square.

"So, *Flick*, huh?"

I smiled and ducked my head. "That's what he's always called since I was a little girl. It's just our thing."

"It's cute." He flashed me a smile. "It suits you."

I nudged him playfully with my elbow, as we continued our walk. "Don't get any ideas." A moment passed. "So, are you riding back home tonight?"

"Yup, I did a quick sobering spell when I visited the men's bathroom earlier. I'm clear of any alcohol."

We were now in the middle of the square, heading towards the direction of my flat. We stopped and faced each other. I looked up at him.

"Mason, thank you so much again for coming tonight.

It really meant a lot to me to have all my close friends meet my dad, and vice versa."

He stuck his fingers into his jeans pocket and nodded. "I had a great evening, too." He paused. "Actually, before I go, I wanted to ask you something." He held up his hands in mock surrender. *"Just as friends*, I was wondering if you'd like to come to Oxford next week?"

"Next week?" I repeated.

"Yeah, it's my friend, Charlie's 30th birthday, and he's celebrating at *After Dark*. Also, Darcey, Mia and Emma know him too, so I'm sure they'll be invited. Would you like to join us?"

"Oh yes, I think Darcy started to mention something about it earlier, but I got distracted so we didn't finish the conversation."

I'd heard about the club, *After Dark,* several times now, and I was curious about all the different paranormal beings that went there. All I knew was that it was run by a vampire called, Drake. "Why not?" I replied and flashed him a grin. "Thanks."

I walked with Mason to where he had parked his Harley. Then I waited until he put his helmet on and started up the bike, releasing the deep rumble of the engine. I immediately felt a craving for wanting to be on the back of the glorious machine again, remembering just how much I enjoyed it the last time. Mason must have noticed my blatant longing.

"I can take you on the back of my bike any time you want, you know?"

I smiled and bit my lip. "I might just take you up on that."

"Are you sure you don't want me to wait until you go inside your flat?"

I shook my head. "Thanks, but I can look after myself. I'm a witch, remember?"

"And a pretty amazing one at that. Good night, Felicity."

I stepped back and watched while he glided off into the night.

I was still wired up after our evening in the pub, and I wasn't quite ready for bed.

*Atticus, are you awake?*

*I am now. What can I do for you?*

*Want to join me for a stroll? I'm outside.*

*Yeah, I guess I could stretch my legs. Open the door.*

I walked over to my flat and opened the front door. Atticus was waiting and slipped out next to me.

"Thanks," I said. "I could do with some company."

"Huh, I thought you'd might want to give your mouth a rest."

I stopped. "Atticus. That's quite rude."

"Not really. Mostly I'm a solitary creature. I can take my friends in doses and then I need my space. Like with you." He continued walking and I caught up with him.

"You're really charming, you know?"

"So Wilma tells me."

The evening had turned out to be quite mild as we walked and I stuck to where the streetlights were, but unlike New Year's Eve, I didn't feel scared. I knew that my powers were stronger, and I wasn't worried for my safety per se. Although I also knew I shouldn't take foolish risks at the same time. As I continued our walk, I reflected on my evening, and again wondered if I could possibly convince Dad over the next few days to consider relocating. Maybe he was warming up to this place after all. Atticus and I strolled in companionable silence.

Soon, I found myself heading in the direction of the police station. I know that they had a small morgue in the basement, and I was fairly sure that Angie's body would temporarily be inside there. As I approached the police station, I slowed my footsteps. I spotted a figure trying to test the front windows, as if wanting to break in.

"Atticus," I whispered. "Do you see that?"

He turned to look up and me and then he followed my line of vision. "Good Gods."

I quickly backed us up into the shadows to watch what they were doing. The streetlights cast a soft glow on their back, which appeared to be that of a man, dressed in full black clothes.

*What in Mother Nature was he doing trying to break into the police station?*

"Felicity, call Desmond." Atticus instructed.

"Okay, you don't think I should see what's going on first?"

"No, make the call."

Without taking my eyes of the man, I pulled out my mobile phone from my coat pocket and called Desmond. He answered on the third ring.

"Felicity? Are you okay?"

"Desmond, someone is trying to break into the police station. I think it's a man. Hurry."

"Felicity, be safe. We don't know if it's the killer."

"I'm across the street," I said quietly and then hung up and watched the intruder who was doing his best to jam open a window.

I knew that, if necessary, I could have shot out a freezing spell on the intruder to hold him while Desmond arrived, but I needn't have worried because Desmond got there in record time. He must have parked further up the road so as to not alert the intruder, and he came running down the street to where I stood across the station. Atticus had moved further back into the bush for now.

"Where is he?" Desmond asked.

I pointed to the open window. "He's just managed to wedge open that window." I glared at Desmond. "You really need better security."

"Not now, Felicity."

Desmond began to cross the road and I followed behind him.

"Stay back, he might be armed and dangerous."

"Don't worry, I'm okay."

We moved towards the front door of the police station and Desmond reached into his pocket and pulled out a key. He placed it in the lock of the door and then we were inside the police station. I stood beside Desmond, both of us listening out for any sound. It was eerily quiet.

"Where do you think he's gone?"

"Headed out back. I told you stay where you are."

I ignored him and followed as Desmond walked forward towards the back of the building. We both spotted the glow of light coming from a torch. Desmond held his hand out to me, indicating for me to stop, while he moved swiftly forward. The next moment, I heard his loud and commanding voice.

"Stop, Police! Stay where you are!"

CHAPTER EIGHTEEN

*I* rushed up behind Desmond and flicked the light switch. The back of the building was flooded with light.

"Okay, okay." The intruder dropped his torch and held up his hands. "Relax, I don't want any trouble."

He was wearing a black jumper, black jeans and a black balaclava which only revealed his beady eyes.

"Who are you? And what are you doing here?" Desmond barked.

"I'm Angie's ex-husband, Jimmy. I heard she was killed here."

I looked at Desmond who had deep vertical lines between his eyes.

"What are you doing here, I repeat?"

"Look, I know this is a small village station, and I heard you have a morgue in the basement. I just wanted to come and say my goodbyes and see what happened to her."

"Stay where you are, and don't move."

Desmond turned and came over to me. He spoke in a quiet voice. "Felicity, thank you for your help, but you're free to go now. I'll deal with him."

*Drats and bats.* I would have loved to have heard more.

"Are you sure you don't need any help?"

Desmond shook his head. "Please go home, Felicity."

I glanced over at Jimmy, who was looking down at his feet. He still had his arms raised in surrender. I didn't think he looked like he would be giving Desmond any trouble.

"Okay, then. Be careful."

I headed away from them and back out the front door. I spotted Atticus across the street, watching from the bush where I'd left him. He stepped out and crossed the road to join me.

"Felicity, are you okay?"

I nodded. "Let's keep walking."

We hurried along the road, until we were a safe distance away from the police station. "Would you believe that man said his name is Jimmy? He's Angie's ex-husband."

"The dead woman? What was he doing there?"

"He told Desmond that he wanted to see her body."

"He's got a thing for dead bodies?"

I looked down Atticus. "He wanted to see her for the last time, apparently."

"Did you get anything else?"

I shook my head. "I wish. But Desmond asked me to leave so I was unable to hear anything else."

We were back in the square by now and we made our way across to our flat.

"It seems suspicious doesn't it, that Jimmy's turned up now that Angie is dead." I said to Atticus as I opened the door. He slipped inside.

"Yeah, I've heard that some murderers like to come back to the scene of the crime to see their handiwork. I wonder if he's one of those sickos."

I shut the door behind me. "I have every intention of finding out."

~

"So, where do you fancy going for lunch?"

I stopped by the *Serene Stay* just after noon and Dad and I were sitting in Lottie's conservatory / breakfast room, catching up. It was pretty miserable and grey outside, in contrast to the cozy room we were in.

"You know what, if you're okay with it, I would really love a pizza."

I waggled my eyebrows. "Well, I just happen to know of a certain Italian restaurant with delicious stone baked pizzas." I shrugged nonchalantly and glanced at dad from under my lashes. "Owner goes by the name of Maria."

I could have sworn I saw a little colour appear in his cheeks and had to bite my lip to stop myself from grinning. I stood up and offered him a hand.

"Come on, let's get you that pizza."

We strolled into the village square and headed for *Buono*. When we entered, Maria spotted my dad, and immediately came over to greet us.

"George," she grinned. "How lovely to see you again."

I side-eyed Dad, who was smiling just as hard. "Well Maria, I guess I couldn't stay away."

"Now, now, you two." I nudged Dad in his ribs.

He cleared his throat, looking embarrassed, and I winked at Maria.

She beckoned us with her hands. "Come on, you two, let's get you fed."

She led us to a table and presented us with the menus. "So, my two favourite customers, what are you in the mood for?"

Dad chuckled. "Maria, I bet you say that to everyone."

Maria looked at him with mock horror. "George, how do you know my secrets?"

We all had a laugh and then Dad consulted the menu.

"I have a craving for a stone baked margarita pizza."

"Well, you've come to the right place. Our dough is freshly made each morning, along with the sweetest of vine tomatoes and the best mozzarella from Italy - well, maybe apart from the Rosgrove's."

"My mouth is already watering." He replied, slapping the menu closed.

Maria looked at me and raised her brow. "Felicity, would you like to try something different?"

"Actually, yes, please. I'm not too hungry, so just a Caesar salad for me, Maria."

She picked up the menus and nodded. "One margarita and one Caesar salad coming up. Sit tight, I'll be with you soon."

As it happened, Maria sent over a selection of bread and olives on the house for us to nibble while we waited for our main course.

"I see you're getting special treatment, Dad," I teased, dipping my piece of focaccia into the mixture of olive oil and balsamic vinegar. I took a bite of the bread. "My gosh, this is utterly delicious."

"It is, indeed. I can see myself regaining my weight ridiculously fast if I stick around here."

The food was lovely and fresh. Towards the end, I got up to use the bathroom and, on my way back, an idea struck me.

"Maria, could I have another chicken pizza to go, please?"

"Are you still hungry?" She enquired, frowning. Maria's hated anyone to leave her restaurant if they weren't stuffed to the gills, and almost took it personally.

"Oh no," I patted my stomach. "I'm very full. It's for a friend."

"Ah, okay. No problem, I'll bring it over soon."

"Thank you," I smiled.

I slipped back into my seat. "Dad, I have to run a quick errand. Do you think you'll be okay on your own for about half hour?"

"Of course," he replied. "I may just stay here for a bit and enjoy an espresso. Everything okay?"

"Oh, yes. I promised a friend a pizza, so I'm just going to drop it off."

Maria came over soon after with the steaming box. I stood up and thanked her.

"Maria, I've got to run, but I'm going to leave Dad here for a bit to enjoy your coffee. Thank you for lunch."

"My pleasure," she beamed. She looked around the restaurant which was fairly quiet. "George, I may just join you for a quick coffee if you don't mind?"

I caught Dad's smile and left them to it. As soon as I was out of the restaurant, carrying the hot pizza box, I sent a message to Atticus.

*Atticus, I'm going to see Desmond.*

*Are you bribing him?*

*How did you know?*

I was back in the square and I spun around, automatically looking up at the window of my flat. Atticus was looking down at me. I held up the pizza box.

*Yes, I'm hoping he'll give me a minute with Jimmy. The pizza may help.*

*Good luck. By the way, you're neglecting me again.*

I winced and continued to walk.

*I promise I'll pick up some roast chicken from Maria on my way back. How come you're getting through it so soon, anyway?*

*Wilma has taken a liking to it too.*

*You're sharing your meals with her? You must really like her.*

*I do. But unfortunately, I didn't expect her to like it as much. I thought she was more of a spring tuna girl.*

I chuckled. *Good luck with that one. I'll be back later.*

∽

Ten minutes later, I pushed open the door to the police station and popped my head inside. I expected to see

Miriam, the usual receptionist at the front desk, but as I glanced around, she was nowhere to be seen. This was my perfect opportunity to head back towards where I knew the holding cells were.

I walked quietly through the hall, looking out for Desmond on my way, but he was also nowhere to be seen. As I passed his office, I knocked and opened the door, but he wasn't in the room. I walked over and left the pizza box on his desk and then I slipped back out, heading towards the cell.

When I arrived, I noticed Jimmy sitting on the mattress, with his head in his hands.

I looked around, in case Desmond was heading my way, but all was quiet.

"Jimmy?"

He snapped his head up. His dark eyes fixed onto mine as I took in his unshaven face and thin lips. He stood from the mattress; eyes narrowed.

"Yeah? What do you want?"

I quickly glanced over my shoulder, and then moved a little closer.

"I just wanted to ask you a question. What were you doing here last night?"

"What are you, another copper?"

"No, I'm not. I met Angie the day before she was

murdered, and she seemed really happy. I just wanted to know why someone would want kill her and wondered if you had any ideas?"

Jimmy's face softened. "She may not have wanted to be with me anymore, but I ain't a killer. Despite our fights, I still loved her. Very much so in fact."

"Well, do you know who would have wanted her dead?"

Jimmy walked towards the bars of the cell and held onto them.

"Yes, I have my suspicions."

"Who, Jimmy?"

He sighed. "Her so-called friend, Molly."

The only friends I met of Angie's were Rose and Clare, so I had no idea who Molly was, but somehow the name rang a bell. "Molly?"

Jimmy pressed his lips together. "Yeah, she helps to run Angie's boutique for her in London."

Of course. Now I vaguely remembered the women discussing whether Molly would be responsible enough to open the boutique.

"If Molly was her friend, why would she want to kill Angie?"

"Look, she's far more dangerous than she lets on. That's all I'm saying."

"But Jimmy-"

"Felicity!" I spun on my heel, and saw Desmond standing there, looking rather annoyed. "What are you doing back here?"

"I was looking for you, Desmond. Miriam wasn't at the front desk either."

"Come on. You can't be back here."

I glanced at Jimmy, who continued to glare at me as I moved away from his cell.

"I brought you food?"

Desmond shot me a dirty look. "You can't just walk into here and start interviewing my suspects. What do you think you're doing?"

I hung my head as we came to stand outside his office. "I'm sorry, Desmond."

He sighed and crossed his arms.

"Jimmy mentioned Molly - Angie's assistant. He thinks she killed her."

"Yes, he does, but he's not all that innocent either. I'll be interviewing Molly in a bit."

"She's here? In Agnes?"

"She will be soon. I called her late last night. She had to look for someone to cover for her at Angie's boutique which is why she couldn't come up this morning."

"Okay, good." I wanted to ask where she was staying,

but I didn't want to push my luck. It was just as easy for me to find out myself. "Anyway, there's pizza on your desk. I thought you might be hungry."

He nodded. "Thanks, that's kind of you. But Felicity, please let me do my job."

CHAPTER NINETEEN

After I left the station, to my slight surprise, my dad texted me to tell me that he was going for a walk with Maria. I knew she closed her restaurant after the lunchtime service and then reopened early evening. Apparently, she was going to give him a walking tour of her favourite spots in the village. I smirked - perhaps someone else had a special interest in wanting Dad to stay.

I decided to go back to my flat and do a little magic to find out where Molly was staying. It would have been easy to ring around the local B&B's but I didn't want Desmond to get wind of it and further annoy him.

"Atticus, I'm back," I called out as I rushed up the stairs of my flat.

"Oh, goody."

I rolled my eyes as I came into the front room to see him sprawled across the floor.

I placed a hand on my hip. "I take it you don't want to hear my news then?"

"Does it involve fresh roast chicken?"

I sighed. "Yes, I told you you'll have it later. I'm referring to my visit at the station just now."

He yawned, and stretched, taking his sweet time. Then he sat up and shook his head, as if clearing it from the cobwebs. "Okay, I'm ready."

I moved across the front room and took a seat on the sofa. "I think we have another suspect in Angie's murder."

"Detail."

I told Atticus about my visit with Jimmy and his implication of Molly, her assistant.

"Now, I just need to find where she's staying."

"How are you going to do that?"

"With some scrying." I got up and went to the cabinet under the TV unit. I reached into the back and pulled out my hand mirror, which was wrapped in a black velvet cloth. I also took two white candles.

Atticus jumped up onto the sofa to watch as I lit the two candles and placed them on either side of the mirror. Then, I sat down on the floor and held the mirror up to my reflection.

I closed my eyes, and took a few deep breaths,

centering myself. I felt the hum of magic as vibrations ran up and down my body. Then, I opened my eyes and looked into the mirror, focusing on where I could find Molly. The current buzzing from my hands connected with the mirror, and it also began to slightly vibrate.

After a few more seconds, I saw past my reflection and a scene began to form in the mirror.

A woman came into view who looked of a similar age to me. She was dressed in a sharp business suit and pulled along a small suitcase on wheels. She wore thick black glasses which were of the stylish kind, and her dark blonde hair was pulled up into a ponytail. I watched as she headed to the B&B, which I immediately recognised as the *Pern* B&B, the same place where Angie's friends, Rose and Clare had stayed. Though I wasn't aware if they were still in Agnes, or if they'd gone back to London yesterday.

The scene began to fade, and the mirror became clear again, once again showing my reflection. I placed it back down onto the table and wrapped it once again in my velvet cloth. The magic in my hands began to subside, and the vibrations dialled back down.

"Bingo." I said to Atticus.

"What's the plan now?"

I stood up and walked over to the window. The square was still pretty busy, with the weekend visitors still in the village from the festival. I expected it would quieten down this evening when they would be on their way back home.

"I'm going to go over to the *Pern* B&B to see if I can speak to Molly before she goes over to meet Desmond."

"Keep me posted."

"I will."

I grabbed my bag and once again left my flat. As I made my way across the square, I glanced around at the people walking through. Could the killer be within the crowd right now?

It took about five or so minutes to get to the *Pern* B&B, and I pulled open the door and stepped inside. Victoria glanced up from the desk, where she was typing on her computer.

"Hello Felicity, I haven't seen you in a while." She smiled, and her brown eyes crinkled at the corners. An assortment of silver bangles jangled on her wrist, as she pushed her hair over her shoulder. "What can I do for you?"

I walked over to the desk. "Hi Victoria. I was wondering if I could speak to one of your guests?"

"Right-o. And who is it you're after?"

"I'm hoping to speak to a lady called Molly, who I believe has checked in recently?"

"Molly Bridge. Yes, she's actually having a coffee in the back."

"Do you mind if I go and have a quick chat?"

Victoria shook her head. "No, not at all."

"Thanks,"

This was a nice place, but Lottie's *Serene Stay* still had the edge. Hers felt a lot more homely and comfortable, whereas this place, while clean, felt a little cold in comparison.

I made my way to the back of the building where, in similar style to Lottie's, Victoria had converted her conservatory into a breakfast room. It was perfectly nice but didn't have the lovely view that Lottie's did of the back garden and stream. I looked around and saw a couple of people relaxing with newspapers and take-away cups of coffee, and then my gaze landed on the back of the lady, who appeared to be Molly from my vision. She was sitting at the table, and held her phone to the side, reading something as she sipped her coffee. I made my way through the room and came to stand in front of her. It took her a moment to register my presence and she glanced up from her phone.

"Hello? Can I help you?"

"Hi, I hope you don't mind me intruding. My name is Felicity, and I just wanted to say that I'm so sorry for the loss of your friend, Angie."

She scrunched her brows. "How'd you know where to find me?"

I casually brushed off her comment. "I was the one who found Angie's body and I heard that you were coming into Agnes this afternoon."

She looked at me almost a little suspiciously, and then set her phone down on the table.

"Do you mind if I join you for a moment?"

She shrugged. "Okay."

I pulled out the chair opposite her. "Thanks. And again, I'm so sorry to hear about Angie. It must have come as a huge shock to you."

Molly picked up her cup and appeared to drain the rest of her coffee.

"It is. I know she'd been looking forward to this weekend for quite some time. Especially since Jimmy, her ex-husband, was finally out of the way so she could be free to do the things she wanted."

"I see. I met Jimmy yesterday."

"Doesn't surprise me that he was here."

"What do you mean?"

Molly shrugged. "Oh, he's always following her around. Pretty creepy if you ask me."

I made a mental note to drop that fact to Desmond. "Did you have a good relationship with Angie?"

"Of course, I did. I was her assistant and she trusted me with her boutique."

I nodded. "Well, do you have any idea who could have killed her?"

"Let's put it this way, while she could appear to be very nice and sweet, Angie also had a mean side." Molly curled her lips and looked away. It seemed that she had been on the receiving end of Angie's *other* side.

"Do you mean how she behaved in her boutique?"

"Yes," Molly answered. "She didn't deserve to die, but there's a few people she's annoyed in her time. Like for example, if someone came into the boutique and looked like they didn't have the money to spend on her clothes, she could be pretty rude to them."

"Really? That doesn't seem nice." I prodded.

"It wasn't. Just last week a man came into the shop claiming he wanted to buy something for his girlfriend, but just because he was scruffy looking, Angie assumed he was there to shoplift. They ended up arguing."

"Oh no. And then what happened?"

"Well, I had to be the one to smooth things out. In the end she went into the back and I was left to deal with the irate man. But all was well in the end, but he swore he'd never set foot in the boutique again." She smirked. "I later told Angie that he could have been one of those undercover millionaires and she could have lost out on a big purchase." She sighed. "It's just an example of how she could be, I'm not sure how you knew her or if at all, but don't buy into all that sweetness and light. She wasn't all that innocent." She pressed her lips together and looked at her phone. "I guess I'd better go and get this over and done with at the police station. I need to go back to London later today."

"Certainly. Have you been in London all this past week?"

Molly fiddled with her phone. "Yes, of course, where else did you expect me to be?" She glared at me.

"Oh, I was just asking in case you might have had any other suspicions about who might have been after Angie."

She stood up and swung her bag onto her shoulder. "Jimmy, he's the one who's always been stalking her."

CHAPTER TWENTY

I contemplated my chat with Molly. I wasn't quite sure what to make of her opinion of Angie, but I didn't fully trust her, and my instinct told me something wasn't adding up.

As I walked slowly towards the square, my thoughts were interrupted when, to my surprise, I saw Becky glancing at the window of *Free Spirits*, Lara's shop. It was the perfect opportunity to catch up with her. I hastened my steps and quickly made my way across the square to where she was standing.

"Becky, I heard you were back."

Becky slowly turned to me. "Oh, hello Felicity."

She didn't seem particularly enthused and turned her head back to stare at the shop display.

"Lara does go all out doesn't she, for these witchy festivals."

I glanced at beautiful nature display in Lara's window. Small trees with dangling ornaments to resemble food, as well as candles set in beautiful brass holders made up most of the scene which was set against a magical background.

"It's lovely, isn't it?"

"Hmmm." Becky abruptly turned away and began to walk.

I chased after her as she sped up.

"Becky, wait. How's things?"

She stopped and once again turned to me but this time she was frowning. "Fine, what are you referring to?"

I was a bit taken aback with how short she was with me but perhaps she just wanted to get on her way.

"I was just making conversation. I hope you had a nice time with your sister in London."

"Yes, it was good but I'm glad to be back. I need to go now."

How very strange, I thought.

～

Once I filled Atticus in on thoughts about Molly, I spent the rest of the afternoon in my shop, working on some new jewellery that I wanted to display for Valentine's Day. I had finished with James's necklace for Mia and was really pleased with how it turned out. I hoped Mia would love it just as much.

Luca's stones would be arriving in the morning by courier, and I was excited to begin work on his custom ring for Lara. I then finished up some paperwork which I had been putting off. All in all, the time passed quickly.

Dad had texted a little while ago to tell me he was going back to the *Serene Stay* to have a little nap and that we'd catch up later. I hope he enjoyed his walk.

I took the opportunity to call Emma, who picked up on the second ring.

"Hey you, we were just talking about you."

"Should I be worried?"

Emma laughed. "No, not at all. We were just discussing *The River Inn*."

"Actually, that's why I rang you. I bumped into Becky a little while ago and I thought she seemed a little strange." I paused. "I was wondering if you guys are free tonight so that we can go and do another reading of the place, as we discussed the other night?"

"Definitely. Hold on, let me check with Mia and Darcey." I heard Emma speaking to them in the background.

"Yeah, Mia and Darcey are in. What time do you want to go?"

"I'm meeting my dad for dinner later, but I should be done by ten. Shall we meet there at that time?"

"Yes, sounds good. Give our love to George, and we'll see you later tonight."

∼

"Thanks for bringing dinner, Flick. That was delicious."

I closed my take-away box of chicken chow mien. I was absolutely stuffed. We were relaxing in his room at the *Serene Stay*, with the TV on in the background.

"You're welcome, Dad. Sorry it's not your favourite *Italian*." I waggled my brows.

Dad chuckled. "Maria's just a friend."

"Oh, yeah?" I grinned and ducked my head.

"Yeah. In fact, young lady, I'd like to know a little more about Mason, but it appears you're keeping your cards close to your chest."

I felt a little heat spread across my face. "He's just a friend," I mumbled.

"So you keep saying. Well, if it matters, I think he's a charming young man."

I smirked. *If only you knew, Dad. Mason certainly has charms in plenty.*

I glanced at my watch; it had just gone nine-thirty.

"Dad, if you don't mind, I might get going."

"I'm not happy about you walking back on your own. Let me come with you."

"No, no, Dad. I'm absolutely fine. Besides Officer Grey has got the main suspect in jail at the minute, so I will be perfectly safe. It's only a ten-minute walk."

Dad shook his head. I knew he wouldn't let me go off on my own, so I had to think fast because I needed to get on my way to meet my friends at *The River Inn*. At that moment, he turned his back, and I took the opportunity to raise my hands and shoot out a quick calming spell through my fingers, which connected with his back. The next second he turned around and yawned widely. His eyes looked heavy.

"Oh, I'm rather tired all of a sudden."

I smiled and stood up. "Well, I'll let you get your rest, Dad, and I'll be on my way." I hugged him goodnight and quickly left the *Serene Stay*.

As soon as I was back out on the street, I opened my bag and pulled out my umbrella. It was drizzling, which was getting heavier by the minute.

*Atticus, are you sure you want to come out? It's raining.*

*Not really, but I don't like the idea of you going on your own.* He sighed heavily.

*I'll be okay, honestly.*

*No, I'll sacrifice my body to the elements. I'll meet you in the square.*

*I'll be there in five.*

*Fine.*

Atticus met me just as I entered the square. I held out my umbrella and he rushed closer to me for cover. As we approached, I saw Darcey Emma and Mia waiting for me just by the side of the bush. An umbrella that stretched across all their heads, was hovering above them.

"Nice," I said, gesturing to the floating umbrella.

"There they are," Mia said, smiling. "Hello Atticus." She smiled at him and then looked back at me. "How's George?"

"Very well, thank you. Thank you all for coming tonight."

Darcey glanced up at the rain, which was getting heavier by the second. "Come on, shall we go in?"

I looked to the left to the main door. "Is it open? Becky in there?"

"I don't think so," Emma answered. "We had a quick look and it's all dark, but the door is open."

"Maybe she's asleep?" I suggested. "Come on, let's get out of the rain." I closed my umbrella, bent down and scooped up Atticus into my arms.

"That's very good of Atticus to join you," Darcey commented. "Ours were fast asleep by the fire when we left. They didn't need telling twice that they could stay home."

I looked down at Atticus as Emma pulled open the door. "Careful, Darcey, his head might not fit through the door."

She chuckled and then we all grew quiet as we stepped into the dark hallway.

I looked around, trying to adjust my eyes to the lack of light.

"It still stinks," I said quietly, wrinkling my nose.

"Yup," Emma whispered. "I don't like this at all."

We crept towards the stairs and climbed the first few steps until the next floor became visible. Then Emma halted abruptly, which caused me to bump into her since I was behind her.

"Sorry," she whispered. She pointed to the door of the bedroom.

My heart sank. A mist was swirling from below the door frame, lifting into the hall and then evaporating away. Darcey and Mia came up next to me and craned their head to see what was going on.

"Let's go," Emma said.

She needn't have asked twice. We turned and swiftly left the building. As soon as we were back outside, I placed Atticus down and took a deep breath.

"It's back." Emma said, with a frown.

"Yep," we all chimed in unison.

"I wonder where Becky is sleeping?" Emma continued. "I hope she's safe."

"Me too. What do we do, now?" I asked.

"I'll speak to Lara in the morning." Emma dragged her hand down her face. "What is this thing?"

Mia sighed and folded her arms. "I think we need to do further research."

"Okay, let's get out of here," Darcey said, shivering as she looked up at the building. "That thing is plain nasty."

～

As Atticus and I walked home discussing the spirit, out of nowhere I was hit with a blinding flash of light. I screamed and fell to the ground, covering my eyes.

"Felicity! What's the matter?" I felt Atticus beside me, his voice panicked.

"I don't know! Atticus what's happening?"

I tried to open my eyes, but I couldn't see him. It was as though I was looking directly into the sun. My eyes were burning, and tears streamed down my face. I screamed again and this time I heard a deep growl from Atticus but then he yelped, falling silent a moment later.

"Atticus!" I called out, crawling blindly on the ground, feeling for him.

Rain splattered against me, soaking me, but I was utterly helpless. It was as though I was being blinded.

And then something grabbed my neck from behind, and a hood was thrown over my head. I struggled and kicked out, but the pain in my eyes was too much.

"Let me go!" I shouted.

"Quiet, and don't do anything funny or you'll never see your familiar again."

CHAPTER TWENTY-ONE

As I was dragged backwards, I felt every stone and bump that cut into my legs and sent pain shooting through my back. As much as I wanted to scream, or blast out a spell, I bit my lips, knowing I couldn't risk doing so until I knew Atticus was no longer in danger.

All of a sudden, I felt a splash of water, and my legs were drenched. There was a sudden change of temperature as I was pulled further along, and this time I knew exactly where I was being taken. Inside the caves, belonging to Queen Cordelia and King Keon. I bit my lip to stop from screaming, as I was further dragged further and deeper through the sharp rocks of the caves. Then abruptly, my captor came to a halt, and I was pushed roughly to the side. The hood was yanked off my head, and it took me a moment before I dared to open my eyes, fearing the pain I felt before. I blinked very slowly and then opened my eyes. Thank the Gods, the searing pain had stopped, and my eyes were no longer burning. It took a moment to adjust to my surrounding, and what little light was provided came from the hundreds of glow worms above me.

"What do you want with me?" I shouted to no one in particular. My captor had disappeared.

I tried to stand, and winced. My legs were in a bad way and I could see my calves were bleeding heavily, from where my jeans had torn. I knew it wasn't a big deal as I could fix a healing spell in a moment, but first I had to wait and see what their next move was. All along I couldn't stop thinking about Atticus, and the fear of anything happening to him, prevented me from lashing out.

*Atticus? Are you okay?*

I waited for him to answer but nothing. Panic spiked inside me.

I blinked as a pair of glowing wings appeared before me. I pulled back and immediately recognised the faerie.

"Shaylee? What are you doing here?"

"Well, I live here, Felicity Knight."

She fluttered above me and began to fly away.

"Shaylee, wait! Where are you going?"

She ignored me and fluttered off.

That was it, I was not waiting any longer, and I moved myself to the sitting position. I was about to stand when a glow of light, almost as bright as what was hurting my eyes earlier, appeared in front of me. I squinted and held my hand up to shield my eyes, but then it turned into a softer hue, and Queen Cordelia and King Keon appeared within the ball of light.

Queen Cordelia was dressed in a flowing white gown and her waist length hair, which was parted down the middle, was glittering silver. She wore a crown of sticks and jewels, which sparkled in the light. Next to her, King Keon was also dressed in a silver coat of arms. Both glared down at me.

"Really, Queen Cordelia and King Keon, if you wanted to see me you could have just asked. No need to go through such a show of trouble."

"I would quieten that sharp tongue of yours, if I were you, Felicity Knight." Queen Cordelia answered. "You should be bargaining for your life."

I gulped. "What have you done to Atticus?"

"As long as you cooperate, he will come to no harm."

I breathed a temporary sigh of relief, but at the same time I knew I couldn't trust her.

"What do you want with me?"

Queen Cordelia moved forward, hovering above me. I craned my neck to look up at her. Her mouth was turned down and her eyes were narrowed.

"There's an unwanted presence in the village of Agnes. It is your fault."

I blinked. I assumed that she was referring to the spirit at *The River Inn.*

"I am aware of this spirit and am doing my best to help banish it. But I've no idea why you think it has anything to do with me."

She laughed harshly and flew back to hover next to King Keon. He folded his arms and looked down at me.

"As usual, Felicity Knight, you are unaware of what is happening around you. It is tiring to continually have to look out for you."

"Look out for me?" I snapped. "I hardly think you kidnapping and dragging me through the night is looking out for me."

"You will not talk to us like that." Queen Cordelia shouted.

I backed up, and as I watched, her hair turned from silver to black. Her outfit which was white turned to a dark green, and she hovered menacingly above me. Magic buzzed through me and I felt the power wanting to unleash, but I fisted my hands to stop from anything escaping. As much as I was tempted to throw an elemental spell her way, until I could get back to Atticus, I wasn't taking any chances.

"I'm sorry," I said through gritted teeth. "Perhaps you can explain to me what you mean?"

"I was double-crossed a long time ago, and I will not have my plans ruined again."

Was the Fae Queen utterly bonkers? I had no idea what she was talking about. Perhaps she had me mixed up with someone else.

"We will do unto you, as we please," she continued, "as your life is owed to us."

"I don't owe you anything," I spat out.

Cordelia pointed her hand at me, and a glittering line of silver connected with my legs. A combination of fire and needles spread through them. I screamed in pain and grabbed my legs as she watched mercilessly. Finally, she pulled her finger away and the pain stopped. I rolled on the floor, trying to massage the pain away from my legs, as tears leaked from the corner of my eyes.

"You do owe us. Don't ever forget that."

I watched as the King and Queen whispered something to each other, and then in a ball of light, they fluttered away. I turned my head to Shaylee, who was quietly watching from the corner.

"Shaylee, help me."

"No," she replied.

"But I saved your life once! You owe me, Shaylee."

I watched as the young faerie seemed to contemplate what I was saying.

"At least tell me what she's talking about? Surely you can tell me that at least?"

"You really don't know, or are you lying Felicity Knight?"

I shook my head, frustrated. "Help me to understand."

"Very well." She fluttered over to me. "Your birth father made a deal with Queen Cordelia. He wanted to have your birth mother fall in love with him, but she wasn't interested."

"Why?"

"He knew that with their lineage, together they would produce an enormously powerful child. So, he came to Queen Cordelia to ask for a fae magic spell."

What?" I gulped. "A spell to trick my birth mother to fall in love with him?"

"Yes, keep up." She snapped. She looked over her shoulder and then it seemed as if she was going to fly away.

"Shaylee, wait. Why, does Queen Cordelia think I owe her? I have nothing to do with my birth parents."

She giggled which irritated me. "Well, Felicity Knight,

if you use that brain of yours, you will see that, by your birth father taking some of Queen Cordelia's magic, you will also have fae magic within you. She wanted to raise you as her own, so she could be even more powerful."

I tried my best to keep up with what she was saying. "So, what happened?"

"You ask too many questions. This is your last answer." She glared down at me. "It seems your mother got news of the plan and took you away."

She moved away to flutter towards the side of the cave, and I knew it was now or never. I had to get away as I'd no idea what Queen Cordelia or King Keon had in store for me. With her back turned, I muttered a quick spell, and threw my hands out. She shrieked and found herself trapped in a ball of ice.

I got to my feet as best as I could and began to make my way towards the end of the cave where I knew there was an exit point. Shaylee screeched and banged on her ice cage and I was terrified someone would arrive to drag me back. I picked up speed and stumbled to the entrance. As soon as I got there, I touched the wall of the cave, and it slid open. I was about to drag myself out when I heard a loud bang. I spun around to see Shaylee had burst through the ball of ice and was coming at me, her face contorted with rage.

"Quick, Felicity. Grab my hand!"

I snapped my head around and saw that Nahla, the nixie who lived by the bridge at the riverbank, was on other side of the entrance. I didn't stop to think and reached out to grab her hand, just as Shaylee was inches away from me. Nahla yanked me out of the cave just in the nick of time as the exit disappeared behind me.

## CHAPTER TWENTY-TWO

I collapsed onto the riverbank and took a few big breaths. Nahla peered down at me with a worried expression.

"Nahla, thank you so much. How did you know I was there?"

"I saw them take you, Felicity. I followed you here and was just trying to think of a way to help you, when I saw you appear at this end."

I sighed. "Thank you, Nahla. If you weren't here to help me just now, I'm almost sure Shaylee would have dragged me back down."

I pulled myself up and looked down at my legs.

"You're cut quite badly. Are you able to heal yourself?"

I nodded. I closed my eyes and rested my hands onto my legs. A current of magic zipped through me and my hands began to glow. I muttered the few words to the healing spell I knew and ran my hands up and down my legs and then rested them on my lower back too. I felt warmth spread into my body, bringing with it healing. After a moment, I opened my eyes.

"Cool spell," Nahla said admiring my work.

"Thanks," I said. I stood up and tested my legs. I was fine. Nahla came to stand next to me.

"What now?"

I glanced around. We were in the back of Lottie's garden at the *Serene Stay*. "Do you know what happened to Atticus?"

Nahla shook her head. "I was more concerned with following you and seeing where they were taking you."

"Did you get a chance to see who my kidnapper was?"

"No, but I assumed it was a faerie from Cordelia's army."

I looked at her gratefully and touched her shoulder. "Thank you again, Nahla, I won't forget your kindness. I don't know what I'd have done without you."

She smiled shyly. "If you're okay now, I'll be on my way."

I nodded. "Yes, I'm fine but I need to find Atticus."

Nahla gave me one last look and floated away. I began to sprint in the direction of the square. I'd never run so fast in my life and made it back in record time. Panting, I came to a halt in the square where the blinding light had crippled me.

I glanced around but Atticus was nowhere to be seen. My heart began to pound even faster as my fear took on another notch.

Atticus, where are you?" I called softly. I spun around on the cobbled stones desperately trying to spot my familiar. I ran around the square, peering into dark areas by the side of the shops, and then I finally spotted a white ball of fur, near *Free Spirits*. I ran towards it, and immense relief flooded through me when I saw it was him. Atticus was lying there, with his eyes closed. I sank down to my feet and placed my hand on him, feeling his body rise and fall with every breath. Thank the Gods he was alive.

"Atticus, wake up."

He didn't respond, so I sat down on the wet cobblestones, and gently picked him up, placing him in my lap. He was completely unresponsive. I closed my eyes and placed my hands on his body, the same way I did with my legs and back. Then I said the healing words and shot magic through my hands and into his body. I concentrated on pouring all my love and healing into him. As I watched, his eyelids fluttered and very slowly, Atticus opened his eyes. As soon as he saw me, he blinked, and his eyes widened. His pupils grew double in size.

"Felicity, what happened?" He attempted to sit up in

my arms, and I helped him stand back onto the ground. He shook himself, as if trying to wake up from a deep sleep.

"The fae kidnapped me."

He hissed. "Felicity, I'm so sorry I couldn't protect you. I think they knocked me out."

I looked around us, the square was deserted at this time of night. I picked him up, and held him close to me, kissing the top of his head. Then I stood up.

"I'm so glad you're okay. Come on, let's get home and we can discuss it when we're inside."

I walked as fast as I could across the square, until I came to the door of my flat and then I entered and shut it behind me. I placed Atticus on the ground, and we slowly walked up the stairs together. Once at the top, I switched on the light, and quickly went over and drew the curtains closed.

Atticus was sitting on the floor and hadn't moved.

"Atticus, are you okay?" I came closer to him and sat down next to him.

He shook his head twice as if trying to clear it. "I think so, I'm not sure what kind of magic they used, but it rendered me useless."

"It's okay, don't blame yourself. I couldn't do anything myself."

"What happened to your eyes back there?"

"Queen Cordelia put a spell on me, I couldn't see. And I didn't dare do a counter-spell because they threatened that they would harm you."

Atticus narrowed his eyes. "I knew it, I've never trusted those fae."

"Tell me about it." I was still reeling from the revelation that Shaylee had told me. "And that's not all."

Atticus looked up at me. "I assumed not. What else happened?"

"First a cup of tea. Do you want anything?" I needed a minute to digest everything.

"No, I'm fine, thank you."

I glanced at him, concerned. The fact that he didn't ask for a snack of roast chicken set alarm bells ringing. I stood up and went into the kitchen, filling the kettle.

Atticus waited patiently while I made myself the hot brew and then I carried the cup and took a seat on the sofa. I patted it and he jumped up and came to sit next to me.

"Apparently, my birth father made a deal with Queen Cordelia and it didn't turn out as she expected. Now she thinks I owe her."

"What kind of deal?"

"It seems that he tried to use a love spell to manipulate my birth mother and had enlisted Queen Cordelia's help in order to trap her." I turned to Atticus. "But why did he need fae magic?"

Atticus hissed. "Because witches and wizards have a hard time getting love potions to work. The heart and mind fight when they aren't in agreement so he knew his magic would be futile. He doesn't sound like a good person."

I took a sip of my tea and placed it back down. I couldn't help it, but my hands trembled at the implication. "Atticus, Shaylee told me that due to the spell from Cordelia, I have some fae in me."

"Well, that would explain why Mason's great-grandfather said he smelt fae on you."

"Of course," I said softly. Did he know about their deal too? "I think I need to speak to Quentin about this."

"And in the meantime, do you think Queen Cordelia is going to come after us again?"

The thought had occurred to me. "I have my necklace to protect us from anything really serious, but I'll consult my grimoire and place a protection ward around both of us tonight. I'm sure my magic is stronger." I pressed my lips together. "There's no way she's ever going to stun and capture us like that again."

I woke up after a restless night of tossing and turning. My immediate thought was that it was strange that Atticus hadn't woken me up as he usually did, raring for his breakfast. I peeled the covers off my bed and padded through the flat. He was curled up fast asleep on the sofa.

I moved next to him and knelt on the floor, stroking his head. His eyes flickered and then he finally opened them.

"What time is it?" He asked, his voice groggy.

I frowned. "Later than normal for you. How are you feeling?"

He yawned. "I'm okay."

I didn't like what I was seeing. He wasn't his normal self. "Atticus, I need to get you checked out at *Creature Comforts*. They're opening today."

He lifted his head. "But why?"

"I don't like what I'm seeing."

"I told you, I'm fine."

I smiled. "I'm sure you are," I said in a soothing voice. "But let's just be sure, okay? I'm not an animal specialist and I couldn't bear it if you were ill, and I didn't know any better."

"Well, if you put it like that, I guess I could have a check over. As long as you stay with me."

I nodded and stood. "Good boy. Now, let's get you some breakfast, first."

CHAPTER TWENTY-THREE

After we'd finished a quick breakfast, Dad texted to tell me that he was going into Oxford to explore for the day. He knew that I had a busy day ahead in the shop, and he didn't want to get in the way. Although of course I would have welcomed his company, I was also slightly relieved that I didn't have to look after him today as I had plans of my own.

"Come on, Atticus."

He still looked quite lethargic, and he didn't finish eating his breakfast, so I knew something was definitely not right.

"You want me to pick you up?"

Atticus stood up tall. "Don't be silly, I'm perfectly able to use my own feet."

"Good, let's get going then before I have to open the shop."

I watched him from the corner of my eye, as we made our way down the stairs, and out of the flat. Thankfully, he seemed to be walking fine which assured me that there was nothing neurological going on. At least I hoped.

The air was fresh from the rain overnight, and the cobblestones were still damp, small pools of puddles here and there. It was chilly outside, and I pulled my coat closer to me as we walked the short distance to *Creature Comforts.* It was just after eight in the morning, but Benedict used to open at that time in case people had to drop their pets in for routine surgeries. As I approached I noticed a light in the reception area. I was pleased to see that the new owner still kept the same time. I paused and looked through the window of *Creature Comforts* but couldn't see anyone at the front desk. The door however was open when I tried it, so I pulled it open, and entered.

A rush of memories hit me. From the moment I first brought Atticus in when I found him by the side of the monument, to recent times of popping in to see Benedict during a spare moment. Sadness overwhelmed me, and I swallowed pushing those feelings away.

"Hello? Is anyone here?"

I heard a shuffle of footsteps, and then a lady appeared in front of me. She smiled. "Hello, how can I help you?"

I couldn't help but admire her glowing and flawless skin, along with her beautiful long, dark brown hair. She looked to be in her early thirties and her deep brown eyes bore into mine, but they were welcoming and warm.

"Oh, hello I'm sorry to be here so early first thing in the morning when I know it's your opening day. I hope it's okay, but I'd like to have my cat checked over, please?"

"Not at all. That's why I'm keeping to the same times as before." She glanced down at Atticus. "What's wrong with your familiar?"

I did a double take. *How did she know?"*

She grinned at my shocked expression, showing a row of perfect, white teeth. "Oh, it's okay, I know who you are. Felicity and Atticus, right?"

I laughed nervously. "How exactly do you know that?"

"My apologies. I'm a dryad, and I live close by, just outside the forest. Erich told me about this vacancy here, and I thought it would be perfect for me. Saves me having to travel into Oxford each day."

Erich was a nixie, who lived by the bridge with Nahla. He shape-shifted into a beautiful white stallion, and I'd seen him a couple of times emerge from the forest, which was close to the bridge.

"So, you're friends with the nix?"

"Oh yes, Erich likes to visit with me in the forest. Let me clarify, I don't live directly inside the forest, but just on the outskirts. As a dryad, I need connection with my home." She paused. "How rude of me not to introduce myself. I'm Aria Skye.

I racked my brain to remember what a dryad was but couldn't come up with an answer. I casually glanced down at Atticus.

*What's a dryad?*

*Tree nymph.*

*A spirit?*

*Yes.*

*Thank you.*

*Welcome.*

"Pleasure to meet you, Aria." I shook her outstretched hand. "I hope you'll be most happy here. I'm new myself, but I love it so far."

"Good to know and thank you. Now, shall we go through so I can take a look at Atticus?"

⁓

After Aria gave Atticus a full check, I was relieved to know that there was nothing seriously with him. She told me he had a slight bump on the back of his head but, other than that, he had a full bill of health. I thanked her and wished her all the best for her first day.

"Well, are you satisfied now?" Atticus mumbled as we walked back home.

"Yes, I am…I'm just happy that you're ok. I guess the fae soldier gave you a little too much of that sleeping spell, or whatever it was. I'll make you a quick potion when we're back to remove any traces of fae magic."

"Fine."

"Fine."

∼

After the courier arrived with my precious stones, I spent the morning in between customers, working on Lara's ring. I was thrilled with how it was shaping up. Despite me thinking that most people would have gone home after the weekend, I was surprised to see that Agnes was still busy. My thoughts turned to Molly and I was just about to call Victoria at the *Pern* B&B, when I glanced up as Regis, my next-door neighbour, stepped into my shop later that afternoon. I lowered my phone.

"Hello, Regis. How's things?"

He pulled his pocket watch from his waistcoat and looked at the time, frowning. "It's gone three o'clock and I've barely had any customers today." He shot me a dirty look like it was my fault, but I was now used to my grumpy neighbour. "What about you, girlie? Have you taken all my customers?"

I laughed. "I assure you I haven't. It's been quiet for me too. Besides, I hate to point out the obvious, but we sell completely different items." I cleared my throat and looked down at my display cabinet.

"Don't you go giving me any lip." He threw his hands at the window in disgust. "You know what the problem is?"

I shrugged and shook my head.

"It's all these tours they've put on for all that hocus pocus nonsense." He gestured wildly with his arm. "They're driving the customers out of the shops and onto these silly witch and ghost tours."

I smiled but ducked my head. He was in a foul mood. And then, just like that he turned around and opened the door. "I've got a customer heading my way. They'd better be in a buying mood."

I peered out the window to where he was looking and to my surprise, I recognised the elegant older lady, with the silver hair, who I'd seen in the pub last week. I took a moment to admire her once again and this time, she was dressed in a lovely navy suit and bright blue blouse. She certainly looked like she came from money, so I knew Regis would pull out all the stops for her.

I smiled to myself and picked up my phone once more, and dialled the *Pern* B&B.

"Pern B&B, can I help you?"

"Victoria? It's me, Felicity."

"Oh, hello Felicity. What can I do for you?"

"I was wondering if Molly is still staying with you? Or has she returned to London?"

Victoria paused for a moment. "Oh, she said she's going stay another night. Although, between you and me, I think officer Grey wanted to keep her around."

"Yes, that makes sense. Do you happen to be aware of her plans?"

"She said she's going to try and make herself busy by joining a tour later this evening. I gave her a few leaflets and she seemed quite interested. Even asked to borrow a witch costume which, as you know, I keep some spare for the tourists. She actually sounded quite excited."

"Fair enough. I was hoping to talk to her again, but maybe I'll catch her later."

"Would you like me to pass on a message to her?"

"No, that's fine. Actually, while I have you on the line, have Clare and Rose gone back to London, or are they still there? I haven't seen them in the square over the last day or so."

"No, they went back to London yesterday afternoon. Poor things. Absolutely devastated, they were. They didn't think they could do anything else being here, but of course I presume that once the funeral arrangements can be made, they'll be back in touch."

"I see. Well, thanks for your help, Victoria. I'll try and catch Molly later."

"No problem, Felicity. Give my regards to your dad."

I smiled as I hung up. Had George charmed everyone in Agnes?

Speaking of Dad, he called to tell me that he had caught up with a couple he met while travelling in Spain. They lived in Oxford and he called them on the off chance. Apparently, they were delighted to hear from him and had insisted on him coming to dinner this evening, so he wouldn't be back in Agnes until late. I was happy he was having a good time.

I decided that while I had the time on my own, it would be the perfect opportunity to visit Quentin and get some answers. But first, I had to message Mason to find out exactly where his great grandfather lived.

CHAPTER TWENTY-FOUR

"Are you able to guarantee my safety, that I won't be turned into a frog or similar? Or worse still, you being turned into an amphibian which would then cause me the hassle of looking for a new witch?"

I glanced away from the steering wheel for a moment and looked at Atticus, who was sitting in the passenger seat. I was pleased that the potion I'd made him earlier had taken effect and he was clearly back to his normal self.

"Why on earth would Quentin Reed want to turn either of us into a frog?"

"Well, I don't know. He doesn't seem to be your greatest fan, so who knows what he'll do to us."

I gulped. Quentin Reed was indeed an immensely powerful wizard, and I had no doubt started off on the wrong foot with him. "Mason told me that he might not be the most receptive, but to persevere anyway."

"It's okay for Mason to say that." Atticus grumbled. "It's not like he'll be with us for protection."

"We don't need Mason's protection. We're perfectly fine on our own."

Atticus turned his face away, sulking, as he stared out the window. He wasn't entirely happy to be coming along on this trip, but I told him it was important to find out about the type of magic that could be inside me, and that as my familiar, he should be supportive. For once he didn't have a smart retort so, here we were, driving to Oxford.

Quentin Reed lived a short distance away from Mason's parents' house, but his mansion was a lot more imposing than theirs. It was white, but the colour could barely be seen through the thick ivy which covered the front. A large oak tree grew in the centre of the circular drive. We pulled up into the driveway, and I turned off the engine, taking in my surroundings.

"Ready?"

"No. It's not too late, Felicity. We can turn around and get out of here. Who knows what that cranky old fool will do to us?"

"Stop saying that." I tutted and unfastened my seatbelt, opening my door. "We're doing this. Come on."

I walked round to the passenger side and opened the door. Atticus hopped out, trailing close by my ankle. Quentin's house was lit up on one side, but the other side of the house was in total darkness. At least I knew that someone was in. I walked up to the huge brass knocker and rapped loudly twice.

"Hello, can I help you?"

I glanced around, looking for a camera, but I couldn't spot one. It felt a little weird talking to the air, but I responded.

"Hello, I'm Felicity Knight and this is my familiar, Atticus Lynch. We're here to see Mr Reed."

"But does Mister Reed want to see you?"

I glanced down to Atticus, confused. "Please let him know that I'm here and I would very much like to talk to him."

"Very well. Stay put and I will check with him."

We waited a few moments, and I didn't dare say anything out loud in case whoever was talking to me was listening in on our conversation. A moment later the door was flung open, and an aged man dressed in a white shirt with long black coat tails and black trousers stood there. His silver hair was neatly brushed to the side.

"Mister Reed has reluctantly agreed to take your visit. You may follow me."

Atticus and I stepped inside Quentin Reed's hall, and I

immediately felt a buzz of magic run through my body. Instinctively I knew this was a incredibly powerful house. We followed, who I assumed was the butler, along the parquet wooden flooring, until he stopped and knocked on a door. The door opened by itself, and he gestured with his hand for us to go in.

"Thank you."

Atticus and I stepped forward into what was Quentin Reed's study. I've never seen such a big oak desk in my life, and Quentin was perched in wingback chair, studying me as I entered. A window ran the length of the width behind him but was covered with heavy, draped curtains. I bet he had a stunning view. To my left, the entire wall was a bookcase, filled with rows upon rows of books. If it were another time and place, I'd have loved to have perused through his collection. A floating pen was hovering by Quentin's side and I cleared my throat and jumped slightly when the door slammed closed behind me.

I bent down and picked up Atticus, bringing him close to my chest. Immediately, I felt him pour his calming magic into me. Quentin didn't say anything, but rather continued to watch us with a hint of suspicion in his eyes.

"Thank you for seeing me, Mr Reed."

He steepled his fingers together and narrowed his eyes. "I'm afraid, my great-grandson would never forgive me if I refused to see you. I'm only doing this for him."

I was getting a little annoyed by his distrust of me, so I lifted my chin and looked him straight in the eye, meeting his steely gaze. "I'm really not sure why you have taken such an intense dislike to me."

I thought I saw a glimmer of a smile pull at the corners of his lips. "You've got fire in your belly. Just like your great-grandmother."

"Well, let me just cut to the chase. I know you're busy and I don't want to take up too much of your time. I was wondering if you could tell me a little bit more about my birth family?"

Quentin relaxed his hands and sank back into his chair.

"Very well. Take a seat."

I looked around, but they weren't any visible seats apart from the one he was sitting on. I gave him a blank stare.

He sighed and gestured with his hand. As if by magic, a chair began to materialise in front of his desk.

"Wait, has that always been there?"

"Wait, you mean you couldn't see it?" He said in a mocking voice.

I pressed my lips together and moved forward, taking a tentative seat on the chair. I almost expected it to disappear and for me to fall flat on my bottom, but thankfully it was very much solid and present.

"Thank you."

"What do you want to know about your birth parents?"

"Whatever you can tell me. Also, going by the last time we met, I know you don't care too much for the fae."

He snorted. "I lost some very dear friends in a battle against the fae many years ago. I *can't stand* those paranormal creatures."

Atticus stirred in my lap and I glanced at him.

*Tread carefully. Or you really will be hopping out of here in amphibian form. I warned you.*

I nodded and lowered my head. "I'm sorry, Mr Reed." I said softly.

This appeared to appease him, and he sighed. "Look, dear, I have no idea what your mother, Allegra, got herself involved with, but I know your great-grandmother Lilly very well. In fact, before she disappeared, we were very good friends."

"I was abducted by one of Queen Cordelia's army the other day. She told me that I owe her. I then found out that she believes that I'm owed to her."

He raised a brow but didn't say anything, so I continued.

"Apparently, my birth father tried to trick my mother into falling in love with him. So, from what I understand, he enlisted the help of Queen Cordelia with a fae love spell."

Quentin's eyes rounded. "So that's why you have the mark of fae on you."

"And you knew that as soon as you saw me." I stated.

"Yes, I could tell straight away. It's a…" he sniffed the air like a dog as if trying to catch my scent. "rather floral scent."

I backed up in my chair and pulled my top up to my nose. "Are you sure it's not my perfume?"

He glared at me and I quickly shut my mouth.

"Is that all?" He asked in a bored tone.

"Please, Mr Reed. I don't have anything to do with Queen Cordelia or King Keon. I have no intention of siding with her if that's what you're thinking. I barely know my own heritage, and I'm still trying to figure this all out. I just want you to know that I don't mean any harm to you or your family."

He didn't anything for a few moments. But then, before me, his expression softened.

"Mason, is very dear to me. I can see now how I might have come across to you when I first met you." He exhaled. "Forgive me, Felicity. I didn't mean to come off as harsh as I did, but at that time I didn't know if you were with the fae."

I shook my head vehemently. "No, I am most certainly not with them."

Quentin Reed started at me and I held his gaze. A

current of magic zipped through me and I got the distinct impression that he must have just performed some sort of truth spell on me. Finally, he appeared to relax. "Very well. Perhaps, we can start over."

I nodded but I had one more question. "You said my great-grandmother Lily, has disappeared. Have you never heard from her or my birth mother?"

Quentin shook his head. "I'm afraid I don't know your birth mother too well. As for Lily, back then, she had gone to Argentina to help set up a coven. Soon afterwards, it was like she dropped off the face of the earth. But we only do that kind of thing when we don't want to be found and there's an important reason for it. I know that when the time is right, she'll be back. Perhaps with your mother too."

"Are you sure she's not...dead?"

"I'm quite sure. Lily and I had a great connection, and I would feel it if she were gone from this world and into another dimension."

I sighed loudly. I was no better off with discovering where they were. "Do you think this fae magic that I have inside me will come to anything?"

"It is yet to be seen, dear girl. But as a descendant from Lily, you will have extraordinarily strong and powerful genes, so I doubt whatever little fae magic you have inside you will ever manifest."

I nodded and stood up. "Thank you again for seeing me." I placed Atticus on the floor, and we walked towards the door.

"Oh, and Felicity?"

I looked at him over my shoulder. "Yes?"

"Do me a favour, and put my great-grandson out of his misery would you?" He chuckled, and it was a lovely, warm, and deep timber sound.

My cheeks flared with heat. "Mr Reed, we're just friends."

"I've been around for a very long time, Miss Knight." He smiled kindly. "And I can tell you this - you two will certainly be together."

I cleared my throat and looked elsewhere.

"Perhaps you'd like to take tea with me, sometime? Now I know you're not with those wretched fae, I should like to get to know my dear friend's great-granddaughter."

I smiled and nodded. "Thank you. I would like that too."

CHAPTER TWENTY-FIVE

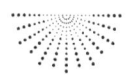

*A*s soon as we were back in the car, I breathed a huge sigh of relief that we weren't kicked out and that the visit went relatively well. I felt I understood Mason's great-grandfather a little better now.

"You seemed to have won him over." Atticus said, settling into his seat. "Soon you'll be drinking tea together like old friends."

"Well, he certainly was like a different wizard at the end."

I started up the engine to the car and backed out of Quentin's drive.

"Do you think George might want a lift back home?"

"No, I sent him a message before we left home earlier but he told he was expecting it to be a late night. He'll get taxi back later."

We got back onto the road heading back in the direction of Agnes. I fiddled with the radio stations until I found one playing some mellow music and we drove on in companionable silence for a bit.

"So, what do you make of him?" Atticus asked.

"Quentin? He seems like a nice man. Of course, if we're going by first impressions, that wasn't the case, but I suppose if he truly believed I was part fae, or there to trick them, I guess he had a right to be suspicious of me. I'm glad I cleared that up though." I shuddered, thinking about Queen Cordelia and King Keon. There was no way in this world or next that I would ever submit myself to her.

"So, Mason, eh?"

I shook my head, then groaned. "Please, don't say anything."

"Well, we know that Quentin Reed is very wise and if he's predicting that you two are going to be together well...watch this space."

I shot Atticus a dirty look. "I told you, and so I keep telling everyone like a broken record, we're *just friends*."

"Yeah, well that record is going to wear out soon."

I ignored him.

As we entered Agnes, and headed towards the village square, up in front of us I saw flashing blue lights.

"Oh, I wonder what's going on up there?"

Atticus sat forward closer to the windscreen. "Shall we pull over?"

I was literally doing that as he spoke, and I stopped the car safely on the side of the road. From where we were, I could see that Desmond was trying to hold back a few people that had gathered around the scene of whatever was happening. My brow creased. Something told me that this wasn't good.

"Come on." I opened my door and jogged around to open Atticus's door. Then we both quickly walked towards the gathering. As we got closer, we saw a lot of shocked faces and a couple of women were crying. My chest began to pick up speed. Something bad had happened. I picked up Atticus and pushed my way through the crowd, until I got to the front and managed to get to where Desmond stood. My eyes widened, when I saw the body of Molly Bridge, on the ground.

"Desmond, what happened?" I said, urgently. "Is Molly okay?"

He turned his head to me. "Felicity." He pressed his lips together. "She's dead."

Molly was dressed in a witch costume, presumably the

one she'd borrowed from Victoria. She would have been on the last tour of the evening, as she'd planned. What immediately struck me was that she had the same red marks on her neck like Angie did, as well as the similar black cord that was discarded next to her body.

"Everybody, I told you get back. Make way! Clear the area!" Desmond shouted.

The small crowd slowly began to back away, and in the next moment, I saw Thomas Townsend, approaching, as he got off his phone.

"Desmond, what can I do?" I asked.

Desmond looked at me and shook his head. "Felicity, this is police business." He turned his head to Thomas, who stood next to him looking puzzled.

"Desmond, it's the mark of that same killer from years back. Look at the way she's been killed. The mark of the cord left behind."

"What killer?" I interrupted.

Desmond leaned closer to me. "Thomas seems to think that this type of killing is reminiscent of an unsolved crime from years ago. However," he turned to Thomas, "it could just be a coincidence?"

"Where's Jimmy" I asked.

"I released him two hours ago, since we didn't have anything concrete to keep holding him. Thomas has just put out an APB - a broadcast - to all police stations in the area to be on the lookout for him. We'll get him back."

My heart sank. Had Molly been right? Was Jimmy really a stalker and a killer? And now the poor woman was dead.

"Desmond, can I ask you something?"

Desmond looked harassed but turned to me once again. "What is it, Felicity?"

"Please, I really want to help. Is it possible to look at those files again of the unsolved murders? Maybe I might be able to find a connection between the killings?

Desmond sighed. "I suppose it might be a good idea to have an extra set of hands. But just this once."

I nodded. "Definitely. And thank you for trusting me."

"The files are in the archives. I won't be able to get them out until later tomorrow afternoon."

"That's fine, I'll swing by the station after work. And if you're swamped, I don't mind giving you a hand to find them."

Thomas said something quietly in Desmond's ear and he nodded.

"You have to excuse me, Felicity. I need to crack on here."

"Sure." I stepped back and watched as Desmond tried his best to control the crowd who were getting close again.

"Felicity!" I spun around to see my friend, Lucy, weaving her way towards me. Her eyes were wide with horror.

"Lucy, what are you doing here?"

"Gareth and I were just having a drink in the Mystical Moon. I heard there was a commotion out here, so we came to see what's going on. My goodness, Felicity. Another murder." She gripped my arm, looking at Molly's body.

"I know, it's just awful."

Lucy shook her head. "What on earth is going on here?"

I leaned in closer so no one could overhear us. "Thomas feels that it's reminiscent of an old crime. I'm going to try and help look through the archives to see if I can find a link."

"Well, if anyone can help, I know you will."

I smiled weakly, flattered by her confidence in me.

"Look," I said pointing to the right of us. "There's Becky. Let's go over and say hi to her."

We pushed through the small crowd and moved next to Becky who was watching what was going on from the side lines.

I tapped her on her shoulder. "Hello, Becky."

She turned to us with a startled look in her eyes. "Hi, Felicity. Oh, hello Lucy."

Becky looked on in horror at the crowd around us.

Lucy creased her brows in confusion. "Isn't this terrible? Two poor women killed."

"Yes," Becky replied, shaking her head. She turned away without saying goodbye and wandered off into the crowd.

"Is she always like this?" I asked, Lucy. "I mean, even before I moved to Agnes?"

Lucy shrugged. "Well, she's always kept to herself, so I don't really know her too well. She's never been one to mix with the locals."

Perhaps I was expecting her to be just as friendly as the other villagers, but clearly Becky preferred to keep her business to herself. Fair enough.

"I'd better go," Lucy said. "I promised a friend that I'd join the last tour with her tomorrow evening, so I'll be around afterwards if you want to meet up?" She turned to Molly's body and lowered her head. "That's if the tours will still be running tomorrow in wake of this."

"Yeah, sure. I'll let you know what I'm doing once I talk with Dad."

"Oh, George is still here? That's great." She waved her hand dismissively. "Don't worry, you carry on with your plans and just text me if you're free."

We both turned to the scene in front of us and I felt a wave of guilt. Here we were making plans for tomorrow and yet poor Molly Bridge was lying dead in front of us and would never see another day. Life was precious and unpredictable.

And I was determined to help find this hideous killer.

CHAPTER TWENTY-SIX

"Mason, to what do I owe the pleasure?"

He entered my shop, and a gust of wind blew in. Mason quickly shut the door behind him. The wind had picked up today and he shivered and rubbed his hands together. I noticed he was wearing a brown leather flying jacket, which complemented his dark blonde wavy hair. His cheeks were flushed from the cold and was it me, or did his aqua eyes appear bluer than ever? All in all, he looked gorgeous. I shoved the thoughts away and went back to cleaning my display unit, in preparation for closing for the day.

"Hi," he smiled. "I hope we're not in for another Beast from the East type of weather."

"I know, I thought we're supposed to be entering spring, and yet it's absolutely freezing."

He stepped towards me and pulled up a stool, perching on the edge. "So, I wanted to call you all day, but I've been busy with clients. I spoke to GG Quentin for about a minute earlier but had to take another call. How'd it go last night?"

"Pretty well, I think.

Mason raised a brow. "Pretty well?

I smiled. "I think he got the wrong impression of me at the start. I discovered that there's a lot more to my birth than what I first knew."

"Oh? Sounds cryptic, Felicity."

"Isn't that the story of my life?" I took a few moments to explain to Mason about my birth father using a fae love spell by enlisting Cordelia's help.

Mason low whistled when I finished the story.

"No wonder he was so harsh with you when he first met you. GG absolutely hates the fae creatures.

"Yes, but once I convinced him that I have absolutely no intention of *siding* with Queen Cordelia or King Keon, he seemed to relax." I shrugged casually. "He's even invited me to take tea with him."

Mason burst out laughing. "No way? Now, you really are in his good books."

I put away my cleaning cloth under my cabinet. "What do you mean?"

"He only invites a very select few into his tea drinking

circle. You truly must have won him over."

"You sound like Atticus."

"Did he say anything else?"

I ducked my head pretending to fiddle under my counter. *Yes, he said we're going to be together one day.*

"I heard that."

I lifted my head, my cheeks burning. "What? I thought I shielded my thoughts." I wanted to die of embarrassment that he heard it. Mason was clearly doing his best to stop himself from laughing.

"Did you tell him you only want to be friends?" He said, once he'd recovered. The amusement had left eyes and all that was left was sincerity. And hope. I couldn't look at him, so I fiddled with my necklace.

"I did," I said softly.

"Good, glad we got that cleared up." His voice had a slight edge to it, and he cleared his throat. "So, I heard about the murder last night." Mason furrowed his brows, and I was glad for the change of subject. "I hope they find this horrid killer soon."

"Me too." I agreed. "In fact, Desmond - Officer Grey - has agreed to let me help him dig through the files. There's a possibility that the crimes are related to some unsolved murders from years ago. I'm heading over to the station shortly."

Mason leaned back on his stool. "What are you, side

lining as a jewellery-designer-come-detective?"

I smiled. "No, not at all. It's just that I've become friends with Desmond, and of course I'm also become really good friends with his sister, Lucy, over the last few months. We have a good relationship, and he doesn't seem to mind too much if I help out now and then. Although there are a lot of initial warnings to *back off, Felicity*. In the end though, I think he appreciates my help."

"Make sense." Mason agreed. "After all, I know you've been instrumental in solving the crimes over the last few months."

"We'll see." I exhaled. "So, did you just drop by for a chat?"

"Actually, I came in for two things. First, you know I mentioned that my friend, Charlie, was having a party at After Dark this coming week?"

"Oh, yes?"

"Well, he's decided to postpone. So, there's no party this week but I'll let you know when the next date is. Apparently, he has his eye on a special lady and she wasn't available this week."

"Oh, that's fine with me. And do you know this special woman that Charlie is after?"

"I do. In fact, I think you'll soon meet her, if you haven't already. She's the new vet who's taken over Creature Comforts."

"Ah, you mean Aria Skye? Your friend is trying to woo her? I don't blame him, she's stunning."

Mason nodded. "So, you've met her? With her opening this week Aria said she'd be too busy to join the party, so Charlie's rescheduled."

"Yes, I met her yesterday, she seems lovely. I had to get Atticus checked over."

"Is he okay?"

"He is, thank you. Actually, there's a whole other story which I haven't told you about. But I'll save that for another day." I think I'd given Queen Cordelia enough of my attention for one evening.

He looked worried. "Okay, as long as everything is okay with the two of you."

I nodded. "It is now."

He still had a look of concern but didn't press me. "Well, the second thing is that it's my mother's birthday in a couple of weeks' time. I was wondering if you would kindly make her a bespoke piece of jewellery?"

"I'd love to. Do you have anything in mind?"

"She loves that necklace you made her so I was wondering if you would maybe make some earrings to go along with that?"

I beamed at him. "Of course, I would love to, Mason."

Mason stayed and kept me company while I shut down the shop for the evening, despite me telling him that he was welcome to go home. After he left, I locked the shop, and then I made my way quickly across the square towards the police station. Atticus had volunteered to come along for a walk, but I knew I would be in the station for a while, and it was cold outside, so I thought it was better for him to stay warm and inside the flat.

As I entered the police station, I peeled off my hat and gloves. Desmond's receptionist Miriam, was still at her desk, tapping away on her computer.

"Hello, Miriam, I thought you would have left by now?"

The older lady looked up and peeled off her glasses. She sighed and shook her head. "No, with what's been going on lately, I'm helping and staying late in case Desmond needs a little more assistance." She pressed her lips together. "The sooner this killer is found and put behind bars the better. I just don't feel safe anymore."

"I agree. Is Desmond in his office?"

"Yes, he is. Go on through, I know he's expecting you." She put her glasses back on and went back to typing on the computer.

"Thanks," I said as I walked towards the back of the police station. When I got to Desmond's office, I knocked on the door, and then entered.

"Hi, Desmond."

Desmond was writing something in a file, and he looked up briefly.

"Hi, Felicity. Come on in."

I entered and took a seat opposite him. "Did you find Jimmy? It's been on my mind all day."

He pressed his lips together and nodded. "An officer picked him up in a bar in Oxford yesterday evening. He was blind drunk and had been there all evening, with witness accounts. It wasn't him who killed Molly. Though from what he confessed, he certainly had motive."

"What do you mean?"

"Jimmy told us that a while back, he'd caught Molly stealing funds from Angie's boutique. When he confronted her, she begged him not to tell, in exchange for passing information to him about Angie's whereabouts."

That made sense. "So that's why Molly said to me that Jimmy was a stalker - she'd been feeding him information all along in exchange for his silence."

"Exactly." He creased his brows. "Do I need to ask when you decided to interview Molly?"

I cleared my throat, feeling a blush appear on my cheek. "It was just in passing," I replied weakly.

"Did she say anything else in that case? Any suspicions as to who murdered Angie?"

"No," I shook my head. "While she said that Angie

wasn't the nicest person to work for, she was convinced it was Jimmy who killed her. She made it out to sound as though Jimmy was obsessed with Angie." I paused. "I'm sorry I didn't tell you I spoke with her."

"Don't tell me I need to put you on my payroll?"

I smiled. "I'm happy to help out, but I'm very content with my shop, thanks."

Desmond dipped his head and looked at the files. "Very well. In that case, please try and restrain yourself from further interviews. Though I know my request falls on deaf ears."

I sat forward in my chair, purposely ignoring his comment. "Are those the files you found?"

"Yes, I had Miriam collect them up from the archives earlier." He exhaled deeply and leaned back in the chair, running his hands through his hair. "Are you sure, you want to do this, Felicity?"

"Yes, I definitely want to help in any way I can."

Desmond gestured to the files. They were three of them. "I know you went through one of them last week when you are looking into *The River Inn*. There's two more there which might give some insight into the unsolved crimes that Thomas was referring to."

I stood up and collected the paper files into my arms.

"Mind if I use the interview room to work?"

"Yes, feel free."

. . .

Time flew past as I immersed myself into the files. I jumped when my phone alerted me to a text message, and I took a moment to breathe slowly before I pulled my phone out from my handbag.

It was a message from my dad asking me to join him at *Buono* in just over an hour. It seems Maria had come up with a new dish and had asked him to sample it for her. I smiled. Of course, I knew he'd be only too pleased to help her out. I shot him back a quick reply agreeing to it and then went back to the files.

When I last looked through the file on The River Inn, there was mention of a patient who was accused of murder. I now pulled out that particular report and went through it once again. It said that the man was called Tobias, and he was accused of murdering two women in the area. Neither women had a connection to each other, but at the time that they were killed, they were both dressed in witch costumes. Like Angie and Molly, these women were also strangled to death with a similar black cord, which had been left by the bodies.

I tapped my pen against the side of my head as I placed the paper report down. This was really odd. There was no other report on Tobias. Where was he now? I picked through the papers specifically looking for him to see if there was any information on his whereabouts, but it appeared that he'd disappeared from Agnes.

So, what had happened to Tobias? The only link I had right now with the present-day murders was what Thomas Townsend had said - that all the victims were dressed the same and killed in the same way. Could it be Tobias once again?

The report said that he was early twenties when he was first accused of the killings, but that was forty years ago. Could he be back?

## CHAPTER TWENTY-SEVEN

"So, what do you think, Dad?"

Dad closed his eyes and finished chewing his food. "That was simply the best Alfredo sauce I've ever tasted." He opened his eyes and lowered his voice, looking around for Maria, but she was on the other side of the restaurant. "Maria said she's changed the recipe - I can't remember what it is she said is different, but it's delicious either way."

I giggled. "You say that about each and every one of Maria's dishes." I reached for my glass of white wine and took a sip.

Dad chuckled. "Really, I wish I could kidnap Maria and take her back to Guildford with me."

I gulped my mouthful of wine and raised a brow him.

His eyes widened, and he shook his head, holding his hands up in surrender.

"Oh, you know what I mean."

I grinned. "Sure, Dad. It wasn't a Freudian slip or anything?"

Just then, Maria came over to our table. She looked at him questioningly. "Well? Put me out of my misery, George."

Dad took Maria's hand and kissed it. "Maria, that was pure heaven. I think it's going to be a hit on your menu."

Maria waved him away and became flustered, but I could see that she was thrilled with his appreciation of her food.

"Thank you, George. In that case I will add the new recipe to the menu from next week." She looked over at me. "Felicity, are you not hungry tonight?

How could I tell both my Dad and Maria, that potentially an old killer was back in Agnes? Desmond and I had discussed it before I left, and he said he was going to look into it and try to track down Tobias. I glanced at my calamari, which was an appetiser on the menu.

"No, not tonight, Maria, I had a big lunch." I felt bad fibbing, but I didn't want to offend Maria, as I knew she took her cooking very seriously. But I was feeling queasy and on edge.

"So, what are your plans for the rest of the night?" Dad asked once Maria had wandered off to serve another customer.

"Nothing, tonight. Lucy had mentioned that she was going on a witch tour with a friend visiting from London, and might be around for a drink later, but that's it."

Dad leant forward and picked up his glass of wine. "What is it with these witch tours? I would have thought it would have been cancelled considering what happened last night."

"I guess, but as you can see, there are tourists visiting Agnes all the time. Yes, it's terrible that a second murder's happened, but the tourists flock here for the paranormal history so it's not as easy as that."

"I suppose I understand. The village makes its money from the tourist trade." He swirled his wine around in his glass. "But seriously, so much fascination with magic and witches. Are you okay with all that?"

Was it the right time to tell my father that I was a witch? I've been contemplating it all evening, and with him due to be returning home soon, I really wanted to tell him and get it off my chest. After all, it was a part of me now.

"Yes." I played with my fork avoiding his gaze. "It doesn't bother me at all."

"You okay, Flick? You've been awfully quiet tonight. Something's up, isn't it?"

I sighed and lowered my fork. "There is something I want to tell you. But can we take a walk? Not in here."

Dad's brows drew together, and his face clouded over with a worry. "Are you sick?"

I reached over and grabbed his hand, giving it a little squeeze. "No, Dad. I'm perfectly healthy."

He nodded, relief washing over his features. "Okay, let's get the bill and take a little stroll so you can tell me your news." He reached inside his jeans pocket for his wallet, but I held up my hand.

"Allow me, I'd like to get this."

He opened his mouth to protest, but I shook my head. "No, Dad."

He leaned back in his chair and smiled. "You've changed, Flick."

I attracted Maria's attention and signalled for the bill. She held up her finger indicating she'd be with us in just a moment. I turned my attention back to him. "How so?"

"I don't know." He smiled. "I told you this the other day - there's this confidence about you now that you never used to have. I'll admit, I'm not totally sold on this village, but I think it's doing you a lot of good. I'm happy for you, darling."

Before I could reply, Maria wandered over with the

bill. I thanked her and gave her the cash, with a large tip. I didn't miss the fact that she told dad she would call him later.

We stepped out of the restaurant, and I slipped on my woolly hat.

Dad zipped up his jacket and tucked his hands in the pockets. "Gosh, it's cold out here, isn't it?"

"They're predicting snow."

"I was rather hoping for some incoming spring weather. Maybe I'll have to go back to Spain."

I glanced at him, feeling a stab of panic. "Would you really do that?"

He shook his head. "No, love. I'm just jesting. As much as it was nice to be away and the weather was perfect, there's no place like home is there?"

We continued to stroll through the square, making small talk and then out towards the little lanes that surrounded it.

"So, what do you have to tell me?"

We had just gone passed the Mystical Moon, and as the stone path temporarily narrowed, I went ahead of him, in single file. This path would soon open out into bigger lane, which would then lead us onto the main road. I was about to answer when I heard a muffled scream up ahead. I spun my head around to dad, my eyes widening.

"No, Flick. Stay behind me."

My dad rushed ahead of me, but I was faster, and I moved in front of him, despite his protests. A hundred years up ahead, under a streetlight, I spotted Lucy who was slumped up against the wall, sinking to her knees. Someone dressed in black, was attempting to strangle her.

Without thinking I threw my arms out and felt magic rush through me like an electric current. Bright blue rays of light shout out my palms and blasted Lucy's attacker away from her. I lowered my hands and began to sprint towards her.

"Lucy! Lucy, are you okay?" She was dressed in her witch costume from the tour she told me she was taking with her friend.

I glanced around for the attacker, but they'd completely disappeared from sight.

Lucy looked up at me, with wide eyes. "Felicity…"

I turned around to see my dad starting at me with a mixture of disbelief and shock. His mouth was hanging open and I watched him as he rubbed his eyes, rapidly blinking as if what he'd just witnessed was from his imagination.

I turned back to Lucy who was sitting on the ground and I sunk to my knees, gently resting my hand on her. "Lucy, can you breathe?"

She cleared her throat and nodded, then ran her hands

over her neck, which was bright red. "I thought I was going to die."

"I need to call Desmond, but I'm not going anywhere." I looked over at Dad who was still frozen to the spot. "Dad, come over here, please? Look after Lucy while I call officer Grey."

As if in slow motion, he picked up his feet and came to stand by Lucy. I dialled Desmond and at the same time, I rushed forward looking from left to right and all around to see if I could spot the attacker. I blasted him hard, but somehow, he had managed to get away. *Fiddlesticks!*

While we waited for Desmond, Lucy had begun to shiver. I knew she was in shock, so I took off my coat and wrapped it around her. She gripped my hand and looked from me to dad, who had barely spoken a few words.

Her voice cracked with the effort of speaking. "Felicity, what did you do back there?"

"I promise I'll explain later. But first tell me, what happened?"

She swallowed slowly. "I met with my friend for the tour, but she had to get the last train back to London, so we only had a quick drink at the Mystical Moon." She paused for a breath. "I was walking this way to get a cab back to Lawnes when someone jumped out at me and began to strangle me. You saved my life, Felicity." She squeezed my hand.

"Lucy, do you recall if they said anything to you?"

Lucy closed her eyes and dipped her chin. "Something along the lines that all witches deserve to die."

CHAPTER TWENTY-EIGHT

*R*apid footsteps approached from the side of us, and we all turned to see Desmond sprinting down the lane to where we were. He came to a halt and dropped to his knees.

"Lucy," he said, his voice breaking. "Oh my God, what did he do to you?"

Desmond pulled his sister into his arms, and comforted her, while Lucy gripped him and began to cry on his shoulder. She did well to hold it together so far, but now the reality of what happened had hit her hard.

Desmond looked up at me, and for the first time, I saw fear in his eyes. It took a few more minutes for Lucy to gather herself together and to get her breathing under control. Then she pulled back from Desmond and wiped her eyes and nose with the sleeve of her arm.

"Felicity saved my life." She looked up at me with fresh tears in her eyes.

I pleaded with her with my own, so that she wouldn't reveal my secret to Desmond.

"Thank goodness," Desmond said, gratefully. "Thank you, Felicity. How did you manage to stop him?"

I felt Dad's stare on the side of my face, and equally, Lucy's gaze penetrating at me. But this wasn't the time to reveal who I truly was.

"I think my dad and I disturbed him as we walked up this lane. He saw us and then darted off."

I looked to Lucy, willing her to back up my story and she seemed to understand, and merely nodded.

"Did you get a chance to see where he disappeared off to?" Desmond glanced around.

I shook my head. "No, by the time I checked on Lucy and then ran up the lane, he had vanished."

Desmond pulled out his radio and barked out some instructions. "All officers in the area are looking for him. We'll get him." He turned back to Lucy. "Come on." Desmond gently pulled Lucy up to her feet as if she were a child. "Let's get you to the hospital."

Lucy weakly protested and began to shake her head. "No, I'm fine I just want to go home. Gareth will be getting worried."

"Don't worry, I'll call Gareth on our way. But I want you checked over."

I hugged my best friend. "I'm so glad you're okay. I'll call you first thing in the morning." Then I stepped back as Desmond led her away down the lane towards his car.

Dad and I walked back to the *Serene Stay* in silence. As soon as we got up to his room, I asked him to sit on the bed while I made him a hot and sweet cup of tea.

"Please, drink this, Dad." I was beginning to think that he was in shock himself.

He did as he was told and took a couple of sips. Then he looked up at me.

"Felicity. Is that what you wanted to tell me?"

I sank to my knees and placed my hands in his lap.

"Dad, I've been wanting to tell you for so long." Tears filled my eyes, as I looked up at him, wanting him with all my heart to understand.

Dad released a shuddering breath and finished the rest of his tea. He placed the empty cup next to him on the bed, and then took my hand and pulled me up to sit next to him.

"Well, I guess you better start at the beginning, love."

I took a deep breath and explained to him about how I'd

arrived in Agnes, and my meeting with Elizabeth Downing who was killed shortly afterwards. I told him about standing on the ley line, and how that triggered the magic within me.

He pressed his lips together. "So, I wonder why your birth mother kept away all these years? It's a pretty big thing for you to find out all on your own."

"I have no idea. I don't know anything about my birth family." I would eventually tell dad about Queen Cordelia and King Keon, and the alleged deal my birth father made with the Fae Queen, but I didn't want to overload him too much just yet.

"So, I guess I missed the invitation for when you turned eleven to send you to Hogwarts," he joked, weakly.

I smiled and threw my arms around his neck. Dad held onto me just as hard.

"I know this is overwhelming and it must feel completely surreal, but this new part of me? I'm still discovering it. I don't really know my powers too well but each day, each week, I feel I'm getting stronger."

I pulled away from dad and looked him in the eye. "But underneath it all, I'm still your daughter. I'm still your Flick, and I always will be."

Dad nodded and wiped a tear away from his eye. "And Atticus, is he magic as well?"

"He is," I said, smiling. "He's amazing, and he's been with me since I arrived in Agnes. He's my familiar."

Dad exhaled. "I guess I'm going to have to get used to all this new terminology."

"It just means that he's my sidekick. We have a great relationship, and we look after each other."

"I see, I guess it's no different to a dog being a man's best friend, then?"

I grinned. I was so happy that dad was taking this well. "Yes, dad I guess it's a similar relationship. Except," I pointed to each finger on my hand, "he talks, he's quite sarcastic and he demands roast chicken on tap." I lowered my hand. "But I wouldn't have him any other way."

Dad chuckled, but then he grew serious. "Felicity, is it safe? This new world that you're part of?"

"I guess I had no choice, dad. The power found me and I'm still getting to grips with all of it. But in terms of safety in Agnes, as you know I have lots of friends who look out for me."

I don't think Dad's eyebrows could reach any higher than it did when I told him that Mason was descended from a powerful line of wizards.

"I knew I liked him." He simply said. Then he yawned, and I knew he had taken in a lot this evening and it was time for him to rest. I kissed him on his cheek and told him I would see him tomorrow.

"Flick, as you know I need to get back home. I'm planning on leaving tomorrow afternoon, but I'll be back to visit in a couple of weeks or so. Is that alright with you?"

"I hate it that you have to leave, Dad. But I understand. I'll also try and come home to visit a bit more as and when I can." I hesitated and looked at him from below my lashes. "Can I ask, is there anything going on with Maria?"

He smiled and ducked his head. "I don't know yet. I just know that we both enjoy each other's company very much. She's, er...she's coming to visit me in Guildford this coming weekend."

I lightly punched him on the shoulder and grinned. "I knew it!"

"Don't get carried away. We're just friends."

I stood up to leave and he walked me to the door. We hugged each other tightly.

"Dad, I'm so glad you finally know the truth about my heritage. I didn't know how you would take it and, in all honesty,, I was dreading telling you." I pulled apart from him. "Thank you for understanding and taking this so well."

Dad took my chin in his hand and looked me in the eye. "Flick, you may be an all-powerful witch-in-training, but just remember I'm your dad. And nothing will ever change that. I'll always love you regardless of whatever life throws at us."

## CHAPTER TWENTY-NINE

As I left the *Serene Stay*, I began the short walk home to my flat. I was lost in thought, as I wandered through the dark evening, hoping, and praying to the Gods, that Lucy was fine, while Desmond attended to her at the hospital.

The poor thing. I knew she'd be doubly in shock from what she'd witnessed this evening with my powers. I blew out a fog-filled breath. That was another conversation I'd have to look forward to. However, I appreciated that she didn't blurt it out to Desmond when he asked how I found her.

Thank the stars that Dad and I had decided to walk down that lane. The enormity of what could have happened to her if I hadn't been there, hit me hard. I could have lost my best friend tonight.

I pressed my lips together and clenched my fists. More than ever, I wanted to find this horrid killer, who was wreaking havoc on the lives of innocent women in Agnes. As I entered the square, I absently looked to my right and immediately slowed my steps. There, lurking in the shadows I spotted the dark figure. Their back was turned to me, so I quietly crept along the perimeter of the square, keeping to the cover of the trees, not taking my eyes off them. The person was sitting down and looking at something on the ground. What caught my eye was the rope that was hanging from their belt. My breath hitched. There was no doubt in my mind that this was the killer.

I moved closer, all my senses on high alert, ready to blast out a spell, when the person must have heard me approaching, and they snapped their head around.

My jaw dropped in disbelief.

*Becky?*

I cautiously stepped forward and at the same time, Becky stood up. She glared at me; eyes narrowed with rage.

"Becky?" I said out loud. I was confused beyond belief. I knew she'd been acting strange lately but now she was just plain angry. Her lips curled with rage.

"You! Always interfering with my plans." She pulled the cord from her waist.

And then it hit me. A series of images like a picture

reel flashed in my mind. The malevolent spirit at *The River Inn*. Becky acting strange and irritable. The murder report from the unsolved crimes from years ago. My stomach knotted with the realisation.

"*Tobias?*"

For a split second, Becky's eyes widened. And then a small smile appeared across her face.

"Finally. Took you long enough."

"Why?" I asked, trying to buy some time and answers.

"Because witches are pure filth! They need to be stopped and no one is doing anything about it. I'm here to make it my mission to kill all of them."

"But the women you killed were innocent. They were merely dressed up in costume, Tobias. You killed those women who hadn't done anything wrong to you."

"Don't tell me that!" He spat at me. "They're witches, through and through, and they deserved to die!"

Becky/Tobias was getting irater by the second. I summoned the magic within me to trap them and magic flowed up and down my body, ready to fire out the spell. I wanted to put them to sleep temporarily, but just before I said the words to the spell, they pushed out their arms, and connected with my forehead. I wasn't ready for it and stumbled backwards, tripping over my feet and falling as a shooting pain burst through my head like an explosion. I try to defend myself, but their magic was stronger than I anticipated.

Everything went black.

~

I opened my eyes and winced at the pain between my brows. I couldn't see clearly due to the thick mist, but I was aware that I was tied up and on the floor. It was freezing cold, and I started to shiver as the cool air slipped through my clothes and chilled my bones. But I wasn't about to sit here and await whatever fate Tobias had in store for me.

"Tobias. Show yourself."

Tobias appeared the next second, in Becky's form. His lips were curled downwards, and he glared at me with contempt.

"Ah, there you are," I said cheerfully. "Though, you might want to work on your hospitality, it's rather cold in here. But then again, I guess you've been dead for so long, you've forgotten your manners."

Tobias rounded on me in a split second, and I felt the sting of his hand as he slapped me hard on my cheek. My head jerked to the right with the force of it.

"Okay, then," I said, flexing my jaw. "So, that's how you want to be."

I tried to move my arms, which were tied painfully behind my back. Equally my legs were bound with the cord he so favoured. I was shoved up against the wall, so at least I had that for support.

*Atticus, can you hear me?*

*Yes, what's the matter? Are you nearly home?*

*No, I'm in trouble. I'm at The River Inn. Please go to my father, he knows the truth about us, and ask him to call Desmond for back up. Desmond will be at the hospital with Lucy, so ask him to dispatch another officer.*

*Felicity, what's going on? Lucy's at the hospital?*

*Please, Atticus, hurry, I'll explain later, but briefly, Becky is possessed with a spirit who has tied me up. I need an officer to cut me loose.*

*Can't George help you?*

*No, I need to disclose what's going on to an officer. I can't protect you and Dad too, so please stay back. Just send the officer in.*

*I'm on my way. Please be careful, Felicity.*

*I'll do my best. Hurry.*

Tobias began to pace the room, agitated. "I've had it with you witches. I told you to leave me alone, but you couldn't stop meddling, could you?"

"So, it's been you all along, Tobias? From early January when Lara and I came here to try and banish you?"

He came closer to me and peered down. "Yes," he spat.

"I wanted to kill you both that night, but you're lucky I spared your filthy lives. I should have ended you then."

"How charming of you. You were rather mean to Lara, throwing her out like that. *Tut Tut*. Unlucky for you she survived."

Tobias moved away and resumed his pacing. I recognised that we were on the top floor of *The River Inn* due to the broken window. Then he let out an evil laugh. "You and your dumb friends thought you'd captured me, didn't you? That stupid witch, Emma, buried the jar in the forest, thinking she'd be rid of me that easily." He threw his head back and laughed. "It was pretty easy breaking out of that, once a fox dug up the hole."

"And then you went to find, Becky in London?" I tried to rub my wrists together to see if I could loosen the cord. I also wanted to keep him talking in the hope that Atticus would get to my Dad any minute now.

"Yes, exactly! She's so down on her miserable life that I found it easy to attach myself to her and bring her back here. There are so many of you dirty witches around here and you must be stopped."

Then, with lightning speed, Tobias wrapped the cord around my neck and began to tighten it.

Fear gripped me and my eyes bulged as I tried my best to kick out and shout for a protection spell, but for whatever reason, I couldn't, and my throat began to close.

Tears leaked from the corners of my eyes as the pressure tightened around my neck. I was choking and all I could see was Tobias's menacing face above me, grinning as he did his best to end my life.

I could barely breathe now, and white spots began to appear behind my eyelids. I was dying and there was nothing I could do to stop him. And then, just as my eyes were closing, there was a blast of light, and Tobias flew backwards, releasing the cord around my neck.

I gulped for air and collapsed on the floor beside me, trying to take in breaths while also attempting to see who saved me.

The mist cleared, the room was flooded in warm light and as I narrowed my eyes, I saw two figures emerge from the light. Even in my half-conscious state, I immediately recognised the woman who stepped forward. It was the beautiful older lady with the silver hair I'd seen a couple of times in Agnes over the past couple of weeks.

"Are you okay, Felicity?" She pulled out her wand and pointed it at me. The cords broke away from my arms and legs. "I'll look at you in a minute, but first we need to blast this spirit back to where he came from."

I sat up and rubbed my neck, speechless, as the second figure stepped out from behind the older lady. She had flowing dark hair and her eyes connected with mine. I sucked in a breath and blinked rapidly. It was like looking into a reflection of myself. Her violet eyes were warm and loving but then she turned her attention to the spirit.

Together, both women said a few words which sounded as though they were chanting in Latin, and then they pointed their wands at Tobias. In turn, his eyes bulged out of his head and I had to cover my ears as Tobias screamed. Bright green light shot out from their wands and hit him in his chest. As I watched, the spirt of Tobias lifted out of Becky's body, twisting, screaming, and swirling, while they kept their wands aimed at him. Eventually, his spirit evaporated and all that was left, was Becky, lying in a heap in the corner of the room.

Both women moved closer to me. I merely stared at them, transfixed, as I tried to take a breath to calm the rapid beating of my chest.

"Who are you?" I asked.

"I'm Lily Cabot." The older lady said smiling, as she bent down to me. "We've met before. I've been longing to tell you who I am." She nodded at her younger companion and moved away to check on Becky.

I looked to the other lady with rounded eyes and my instinct told me I knew who she was before she confirmed it.

"At last," Her open smile was warm and loving as she reached out to me and gently touched my face. At the same time, the burning in my throat immediately passed. I swallowed easily.

"Hello, darling. I'm Allegra." Tears filled her eyes and openly spilled down her face. She lowered her eyes to my neck. "I'm so happy to see that my dear friend, Elizabeth, gave you my necklace. It looks lovely on you. Gods rest her soul."

Completely overwhelmed, I couldn't stop myself as my tears also began to flow. "You're my mother?"

"Yes, Felicity. I've yearned to meet you again for so long. But your birth father is extremely dangerous - don't ever forget that. For now, it has to be this way as we need to protect you from afar."

I brushed away my tears. "So, it's you that's been sending me those mysterious notes?"

Her forehead tightened. "The only thing I sent you was the grimoire."

At that moment, there was a great loud bang, and I knew the sound was the door to *The River Inn* being smashed open.

"Felicity!" Desmond's voice roared, and then I heard his footsteps pounding up the stairs.

The light around my mother and great-grandmother began to fade.

"No!" I cried, fresh tears filling my eyes. "Please, don't go...wait…"

I had questions, but Allegra looked at me with so much pain in her eyes that Lily took her hand.

"We'll see you again, soon, darling," Lily replied. "Becky will be fine, and so will you."

"Please!" I called, reaching out with my hands as if I could grab onto their light.

And then, as Desmond burst into the room slamming the door back on its hinges, their light vanished.

CHAPTER THIRTY

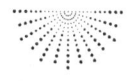

*I* lowered my head and brushed away my tears.

"Felicity, what happened?" Desmond rushed across to me and dropped to his knees.

I looked up and saw his anguished face. I was fairly sure mine reflected the same.

"Desmond, I thought you'd be at the hospital with Lucy?"

"They checked her over and then gave her a sedative so she's sleeping now. I got a call from your father telling me you're in trouble, so I rushed over."

"Thank you."

He looked across to the room where Becky was still sleeping in the corner. He got up and moved over to her, gently shaking her. "Becky, are you okay?"

"She's fine," I replied, softly. "But she hasn't been

herself."

"What do you mean?"

Desmond looked from me to Becky, his brows deeply creased.

"Desmond, I think you better sit down. I've got something to tell you."

He exhaled loudly. "Okay. Talk to me, Felicity."

I glanced up at the ceiling. Mould covered it in thick patches. The mist had all gone and so had the freezing air. The temperature was normalising.

"I will, but you have to hear me out without interrupting."

"Done." He moved over and pulled up a chair. I remained where I was on the floor, but drew my legs up to me, hugging my knees.

"Desmond, there are things in this world that you're not aware of." I looked at him, but he kept his expression neutral. For now. I took a deep breath. "Becky has been possessed for some time now. She's been the killer all along, but it wasn't her doing."

"What?" Desmond's mouth dropped open.

I held up my hand. "Let me continue, please." He gave me a curt nod, so I went on. "When I was looking though the files of *The River Inn*, I read up on the unsolved murders that Thomas talked about. A man called Tobias was suspected of killing three women, but there wasn't enough evidence to convict him, so he walked free. But, as Thomas rightly said, the victims then and now were all strangled, with the similar type of cord and under the same circumstances."

"Yes, go on." He gestured with his hand impatiently.

"Well, Tobias died but his spirit came back to finish the work he couldn't during his lifetime. You see, Tobias hated women who he thought were witches. And as most of the women who take the tours of the village dress up in witch costumes, Tobias wrongly believed they were real witches. He set out to kill them all, including me and others."

'Oooookay." His tone was a mixture of disbelief and anger. "I wasn't born yesterday, Miss Knight. And what's it to do with you?"

"Look, I know this is hard to comprehend, but it's the truth." I lowered my head. "And you should know that I'm a real witch."

Silence filled the room as Desmond contemplated my words. His facial expression went from shock to contempt. Then he burst out laughing.

"Please, spare me the nonsense, Felicity." He stopped laughing and his tone hardened. "Look, tell me the truth now or I'll have no choice but to take you in. I'm not messing about, Felicity. What happened to Becky?"

I shook my head and my eyes pleaded with his.

"Desmond, I promise I'm not lying. I only found out about my birth parents when I arrived in Agnes. I'm telling you, I'm a witch and that there are other paranormal beings in Agnes, but I'm not at liberty to disclose who they are."

Desmond sighed and dragged his hand down his face. "Right, that's it. I'm sorry to do this after the night we've had, but I'm going to have to take you in to the station. Perhaps after a night in the cell, you'll come to your senses and tell me the truth."

He stood and went to reach for me, but I raised my hands in front of me. A wind began to swirl in the room, getting stronger and stronger until the strength of it was physically pushing Desmond back from me. His eyes were as big as saucers, his hair flying backwards, as he pushed out his hands to steady himself.

I lowered my hands and the wind dissipated until the room was the same temperature as before. Desmond looked from me to my hands.

"What did you just do?" He whispered.

"I'm new at this but I can control some of the elements."

"Do it again."

I was worn out and tired and my magic was weak, but I summoned the strength inside me to do it once again. Then I dropped my hands and closed my eyes for a moment.

Desmond's knees buckled from underneath him and he sank to the floor.

"I'm a man of hard evidence and facts, but what I just saw…it was…"

"Magic," I finished for him, opening my eyes. I was so very tired now. "That's how I saved Lucy earlier…I blasted the killer - Tobias - away from her."

Desmond nodded and I could almost see his brain turning as he tried to make sense of what he saw. In the corner of the room, we heard a groan and we both turned to Becky, as she carefully sat up, rubbing her eyes.

I held my breath as she looked from me to Desmond.

"Desmond? Felicity? What are you doing here?" She shook her head as if waking up from a deep sleep.

"Are you alright, Becky?" Desmond asked, moving over to her and holding out a hand.

She nodded her head, though her expression was full of confusion. "I don't understand, I was in London with my sister…how did I get here?"

Desmond cast me a glance and I gave him a slight nod. She had no idea she'd been possessed by Tobias. Whatever spell my great-grandmother and mother did, it had worked, and Tobias was gone for good.

"It's okay, Becky. You're just a little confused," I said, standing and moving over to her.

"I think I should like to go to bed, if you two don't

mind?" She took Desmond's hand and stood up, looking suspiciously at us.

We moved out her way as Becky stumbled out of the room and down the flight of stairs.

Desmond looked at me for a long minute. "So, if what you're saying is true-?"

"-it is," I interrupted.

"If what you're saying is true," he continued, "then I can't charge Becky as she will have had no idea about the murders." He pressed his lips together.

"What are you going to do?" I asked.

He shook his head and went to the window to look out. "Your dad is standing down there. You may want to go and tell him you're ok."

"I will. But what about you, Desmond? Are you okay?"

He shrugged. "This is a lot to take in." He moved from the window and came to stand by me. "I'm not sure how I feel about it but...you're telling the truth, aren't you? I mean, I can see you're magical - a witch as you put it - but all this talk of possession..." He genuinely looked bewildered, and I placed a hand on his shoulder. At the same time, I passed some calming magic to him so that he'd be able to think clearly.

"Felicity, I don't know how I'm going to close this case since paranormal activity has been involved...but I have to ask you one thing."

"Please do."

"Can we keep this magic revelation between us? I don't think it would be in your favour to reveal it to the villagers."

I widened my eyes. "Of course. And that's exactly how I want it to stay…Desmond, I had no choice but to reveal my true self to you." I hesitated. "And earlier, Lucy."

"Lucy knows too?"

"She saw me when I threw a spell at Tobias to get him away from her."

Desmond gulped. "You saved her life…" He shook his head and looked elsewhere. "I don't know, what I'd have done if…" his voice broke, "…if anything happened to my sister."

Tears filled his eyes and impulsively, I pulled Desmond to me and gave him a hug.

"She's going to be okay," I said soothingly.

We pulled apart and he roughly brushed at his tears. "Go on, off you go or your Dad will be blasting through this place next." He gave me a small smile.

I walked towards the door and then turned back around. "Thanks for coming, Desmond. I'm really glad it was you and not one of your other officers that I would have had to reveal myself to."

He nodded. "Me too."

EPILOGUE

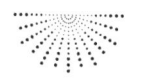

A week had gone past since the eventful night at *The River Inn,* and I was currently sipping a glass of champagne at Luca Rossini's house, in Lawnes.

Darcey moved closer to me. "Isn't this house amazing? I wish we could afford something like this."

We both glanced around Luca's kitchen with amazement. His home was everything I expected from the polished, werewolf shifter. Ultra-modern and slick, airy, bright and minimalist. Lots of lovely textures and clean lines.

We were gathered in his kitchen on a Sunday afternoon for a barbecue, despite the cool February temperature. Luca laughed it off saying that the weather was actually mild for him and his pack.

"How's the house hunt going? Sorry I haven't asked in a while, I've been preoccupied."

Darcy gave me a sympathetic smile. "Still looking, but please don't apologise, after everything you've been through. Do you have any news on Officer Grey's decision?"

I nodded. I wasn't sure how things would be after I disclosed my secret to him, but I needn't have worried. "Yes, he told me yesterday that he's closing the files and marking them as unsolved."

"And Becky?"

"He's not pressing charges as he realises that she was possessed. Hard as it was for him to get to grips with it, I'm impressed that he seems to have taken it all in his stride."

"That's great. It could have gone the other way. But you had no choice."

I shook my head. "I didn't. I had to absolve Becky, so it was the only way."

Mia joined us. "Have you seen Becky around?"

I shifted my weight, so I was also facing Mia. "Yes, she seems fine, though a little miffed about the state of her B&B. She can't understand how it's got into such a bad state. I feel awful for her as she thinks she's going mad, but she can't explain the mould among other things."

I looked up and smiled at Emma who had also moved next to us. "I think we have a solution for that."

"We do?" I raised a brow.

"We do. I spoke to Lara and she's agreed to do a cleaning spell. We'll tell Becky that we want to help and get her out of there for the day. And then, we'll go in and work our magic."

I grinned. "No pun intended. That's great."

"How's George?" Mia asked. "Is he coming back to visit soon?"

"Yes, we've agreed to make it so that we see each other every other weekend. I feel that somehow, through all this, we've become even closer." I was always close to my Dad but now I felt we had an even stronger connection.

I felt a tail wrap around my legs, and I looked down to see Atticus looking up at me. I bent down and scooped him up.

"Hey you, I thought you were hanging out with Blaze."

"There's too much food around and I don't trust his clumsy ways. I'm still affected by what happened to me in Lara's shop."

I bit back a grin and petted his head. Then my arm began to ache. "Atticus, we need to slow down on the roast chicken. I swear you're a few pounds heavier."

Atticus pulled back from me and widened his eyes.

"How very rude of you. Wilma hasn't said anything of the sort to me, so I think you're just being mean."

"I'm not! I care about you and I want you to live a long and healthy life…and that may mean you might want to watch your weight? Just a teeny tiny bit?"

"Please lower me immediately. I won't stand here and be privy to your barrage of insults."

"Atticus…"

He wriggled out of my arms and I put him down before he jumped. Then he waddled off into the crowd with his tail puffed up and high in the air.

Ooops.

∽

"Ladies and gentlemen, can I have your attention for just a moment, please?"

I'd been chatting to Mason who was standing next to me and we all quieted down as Luca made his announcement. As I watched, he grabbed Lara's hand from the crowd and brought her closer to him. She looked on with surprise and waggled her brows which made the guests laugh. I smiled and spotted Mia who had her arms wrapped around James. They'd finally got back together a few days ago and she was wearing the necklace I made that he'd gifted her. He told me that she absolutely loved it.

"Thank you, everyone." Luca turned to Lara and his eyes were shining. He took her hand in his and then slowly lowered himself onto one knee. My breath hitched as silence fell over the room.

"Lara Rose Motley. I loved you from the moment I saw you when your car rear-ended mine." A few of his shifter friends started to laugh and Luca grinned. Then he held up his hand and it was pin-drop silent. "From the second I saw you; I knew you were the one. As you know, wolves mate for life, and you are part of me, my soul." He took a breath. "I know I'm no fancy wizard, but I promise to make each day with me even more magical than the last. I love you, Lara." He paused. "Will you marry me?" Luca pulled out the ring box from his pocket and Lara threw her hands over her mouth in surprise.

"Yes," she said softly. "Yes! I'll marry you, Luca Rossini!"

I released the breath I didn't know I was holding, and tears filled my eyes as we all clapped and cheered for them. Luca rose from the floor, slipped the ring onto her finger, and picked Lara up into a bear hug, pressing his lips to hers.

I laughed and turned to Mason, who was also grinning. Then he looked at me and our eyes locked. For that second, everything faded away into the background and it was just Mason and I. Unintentionally, my gaze lowered until they fell on his lips and in my mind, I heard Quentin's prediction about us.

A loud scream of joy interrupted us, and I jerked my head away to see Lara showing off her ring to the women who had gathered around her. I looked up at Mason and cleared my throat.

"Excuse me," I said as I made my way over to Lara.

Lara pulled me out from the back and showed off her ring.

"Felicity, I absolutely love it."

I grinned. It was perfect for her. "How did you know it was me?"

"It's stunning and unique, just like you." She pulled me into a fierce hug. "Thank you."

"You're so welcome. Congratulations."

She pulled apart from me, her face shining with joy. "Eeeeek! I have a fiancé now!"

I laughed and nodded. "You do. I do have a question, though?"

"Sure, what is it?"

"I was wondering when you both have children...will they be…"

"Magical or were babies?"

I nodded, shyly. "I wasn't sure if it's okay to ask."

"Of course it is, you can ask me anything. Now, there is no straight answer to that I'm afraid. It's the luck of nature - we could either have witches or werewolf babies. And even if we have girls, there's no guarantee that they'll have my magical abilities."

"So, it's all down to genetics like in human conception."

"Yes, just whatever is stronger at the time. Now, if we were to have a hybrid baby - that's a half magical, half were baby, then they would be an exceedingly rare paranormal." She smiled. "But I know we'd love whatever Mother Nature blessed us with."

I gave her another hug. "I think you'll both be incredible parents when the time comes."

As the celebrations of the afternoon continued into the evening, I decided to leave and walk the short distance home. Mason caught up with me just as I finished saying my goodbyes. Atticus was still sulking and told me a little while ago that he was going to visit Wilma. I told him to have a good time. I'd been in a melancholy mood for days and didn't mind being by myself.

"Felicity? Do you want a ride home?"

I was standing outside Luca's house and eyed up

Mason's Harley. I chewed on my lips as I contemplated the decision.

"Are you sure?" I couldn't resist after all. Perhaps a ride would shake me out of my funk.

"Yeah. I wouldn't have asked otherwise." He moved over to the bike and passed me the spare helmet. I slipped it on, and then climbed on behind him.

"Are you ready?"

"Yes."

"Hold tight."

I slipped my arms around his waist and Mason started up the mechanical beast. The engine roared to life and then we were off.

Mason leaned his head back and shouted above the noise. "You want to take a longer route home?"

How did he know it was just what I needed? "Yes," I shouted back.

I placed the side of my head against his back as we rode along the country roads, enjoying the freedom of the open road and the wind in my face. I couldn't tell if it was the wind or my emotions, but soon my face was wet with tears. I closed my eyes and swallowed, pushing away my thoughts, and did my best to enjoy the ride, but the tears wouldn't stop flowing. I lost track of time, absorbed in my thoughts until Mason slowed down and I realised that we were outside my flat. Mason switched off the engine and I released my grip on him. He slid off the bike and offered me his hand. Without a word, I placed my hand in his and swung my legs off the bike. Then I peeled off my helmet.

I knew he could tell I'd been crying, and I didn't try to stop the tears which just seemed to want to keep leaking.

"Oh, sweetheart. Come here."

He pulled me into his arms and held me tight, stroking my hair. I don't know how long we stood there for, but eventually, I felt the heaviness release from my chest, and I gently moved away.

"Thank you." I whispered.

"Have you seen them again?" He asked.

I shook my head and looked at the ground. "No."

I'd told Mason about seeing my great-grandmother and mother that night at *The River Inn*. He told me that Quentin was overjoyed that Lily was back in the picture, but the truth was, they weren't. They appeared and gave me hope for a fleeting moment and then they were gone again. And I was alone once more. I loved my Dad, but he was adamant his life was in Guilford and he wasn't a paranormal either. Lately, I'd felt terribly alone in all this and I had begun to question if I'd really seen Lily and Allegra, or if it was just my imagination.

"The time isn't right, Felicity."

I snorted and crossed my arms. "It never is for them, is it?"

I sighed and looked at Mason. It wasn't his fault I was feeling this way. I reached up and placed a soft kiss on his cheek.

"Thank you for always being here for me."

Mason was inches away from my face. "Felicity…" His expression was torn. I knew he wanted to kiss me, but he was battling with himself to just be my friend.

"I'm sorry, Mason." I stepped away. "Perhaps it's best if you forget about me."

"No! I could never do that."

Fresh tears filled my eyes. "Maybe you should. There's obviously something very wrong with me that my mother and great-grandmother can't stand." I threw my hands out and laughed bitterly. "I mean, look at me, Mason! What's so wrong with me that they can't even bear to be near me?"

Mason's face was anguished as he reached out for me, but I shook my head and stepped away.

As I walked to the door of my flat, with my head held high, I felt Mason's eyes on me, but it was better for him to make a life of his own. I didn't want to drag him down with me.

I made a decision then and there.

Since my real mother had no interest in helping me, I was going to get answers and the full truth about my birth parents from the Fae Queen.

I didn't ask for this life, and I was sick of waiting around.

It was time to take matters into my own hands.

**Looks like Felicity is on a mission! Along with her beloved Atticus, are you ready to find out what's next?**

Buy your copy of **A Not So Purrfect Spell** to keep reading this series today!

COMING NEXT

***The cat will soon be out of the bag. Watch out for some serious claws.***

Having uncovered her biological parents' chaotic history, Felicity Knight now understands her own latent powers far better than ever, but where is the love-potion lovechild of a witch and warlock to go in this world? When someone from her past returns, she'll need to make a tough decision: believe in second chances or embrace her mother's advice to run.

Life is never easy. Felicity finds herself compelled to help Darcey deal with a dastardly ex, Atticus with a much-resented diet, and Desmond with yet another attack. At first, the case is a big "dead end," but one fact slowly comes to light: the victim was working for the kind of people that don't have time or patience for moral dilemmas.

As Felicity digs herself deeper, she'll be forced to consider where her true alliances lie. To solve dual mysteries, divert disaster, and finally resolve her feelings for Mason, will call for a whole lot of magic...

*A Not So Purrfect Spell* **is now available. Scan the QR code below to take you to Amazon:**

LET'S BE FRIENDS

I'd love to keep in touch with you. Please join my newsletter where you'll be able to get a free prequel to book 1, A Not So Purrfect Murder.

Scan the QR code below to take you to my signup page:

LET'S BE FRIENDS

You can find me on Facebook:

D Watts Cozies

Don't forget to leave a review on Amazon so that other readers can find my books. Thank you!

Made in the USA
Monee, IL
18 October 2021